D0130686

CODENAME **QUICKSILVER**

End Game

Look out for the other
CODENAME **QUICKSILVER** books

CODENAME
QUICKSILVER

End Game

Allan Jones

Orion
Children's Books

With special thanks to Rob Rudderham.

First published in Great Britain in 2013
by Orion Children's Books
a division of the Orion Publishing Group Ltd
Orion House
5 Upper St Martin's Lane
London WC2H 9EA
An Hachette UK company

1 3 5 7 9 10 8 6 4 2

The Orion Publishing Group's policy is to use papers that are natural,
renewable and recyclable products and made from wood grown in
sustainable forests. The logging and manufacturing processes are expected
to conform to the environmental regulations of the country of origin.
A catalogue record for this book is available from the British Library.

ISBN 978 1 4440 0550 9

Printed in Great Britain by Clays Ltd, St Ives plc

For Isabel – but also for Kiki, Maria, Sami and Jamie

CHAPTER **ONE**

THE ATLAS MOUNTAINS. MOROCCO.
LATITUDE: 32.361403°
LONGITUDE: -1.977539°

Zak Archer lay flat on a high ridge overlooking the ruined old Foreign Legion fort of Jebel Lekst. The sun was just rising over the parched landscape of rock and scrub, throwing sharp-edged shadows over the broken peaks and deep canyons of the Atlas Mountains.

Zak glanced to his left. Switchblade was hunkered down about twenty metres away. Further off, where the ridge curved towards the fort, he could make out Moonbeam's red hair between two jagged fingers of rock. To the right, Jackhammer and Wildcat were waiting for the word.

Switch was group leader on this operation. The five of them had travelled all night to get here, bumping along a narrow earth track in their Range Rover, headlights off to lower the risk of them being spotted from the air or from distant peaks. Moonbeam had been at the wheel. She was trained to drive anything with wheels or wings.

At fourteen years old, Zak was the youngest of the group; Wildcat was fifteen, the others were all sixteen. But they were all skilled agents in the specialist department of British Intelligence called Project 17. And they had a vital mission to perform in this inhospitable landscape. The fate of the world might well rest on them getting it right.

Zak turned back to the fort. It was brown, with a rectangular outer wall surrounding a group of low, square buildings. It almost looked like an elaborate sandcastle that had been left to crumble away in the sun. He put the Hotscope binoculars to his eyes again and immediately all the colours and shapes morphed into a weird pattern of blues and pale greens.

He was scoping for orange or red.

The blue-green end of the colour spectrum meant cold, lifeless. Orange-red showed heat and life. They'd had to be here early for this. Once the sun began to beat down on the valley, everything would turn furnace-red and there would be no chance of spotting a body moving about.

Zak roved his Hotscope over the buildings.

Nothing.

Now what? Would Switch order them to advance and hope for the best? What if the German agent codenamed Isabel wasn't there any more? What if their intel was wrong and she'd never been there?

He let out a sharp breath. A small splinter of red had appeared from behind one of the buildings – just for an instant. Then it had vanished again.

"Target acquired," Zak murmured, knowing the microphone of the Imp in his ear would relay his words to all his fellow agents. The Imp was an extraordinary new piece of kit: no bigger than an earplug, it contained a microphone and receiver that gave pinpoint reception up to five hundred metres.

"Where?" Switch's voice came in his ear.

"Front right building," said Zak, his heart starting to beat faster, his body tingling and ready for action. "Someone poked their head out from behind then disappeared again."

"Certain?" asked Switch.

"You bet," said Zak.

"Okay, guys," came Switch's voice again. "We're moving in. Keep to cover. Moon and Hammer, I want you round the back. Cat and I will take the sides. Silver, in through the front, okay?"

"Got it," said Zak. His codename was Quicksilver. The name suited his particular abilities, as he imagined Isabel was about to find out.

One by one the heads of the others drew back. Zak shuffled forwards on elbows and knees, peering down the steep drop, plotting a way down. A kind of rough-edged fissure ran sideways down the cliff-face, like a scar. The perfect cover.

He scrambled over the brink and slithered into the narrow groove. He made his way down the cliff, then, darting from boulder to boulder, he sped towards the fort's half-ruined gateway. The gates were long gone and one of the towers had fallen in on itself.

He caught a glimpse of Switch racing across the sand to his left.

He paused for a moment in the cool shadow of the gateway tower. There was about ten metres of open ground between him and the entrance to the building where he'd seen the red image.

Stealth wouldn't help him now; he needed speed.

Taking a single deep breath he broke cover and ran for the dark oblong of the doorway. He was in the zone in an instant – in that amazing place where his mind and his body locked together and he could outrun the wind.

He was through the doorway in moments, moving smoothly and effortlessly, feet kicking up the dust, arms moving like pistons at his sides.

The light was dim and grainy in the building as he ran from room to room.

He found her crouching in a back room, dressed in desert camouflage fatigues, a peaked cap low over her eyes, a backpack on her shoulders. He had a brief impression of large black eyes and shoulder-length black hair. But the thing that stopped him for a moment was how young she looked.

Colonel Hunter had told them Isabel was in her teens – but it had never occurred to Zak that she might be no more than his age. Apart from twelve-year-old Bug, the computer genius back in Fortress, Zak was the youngest agent in Project 17. Did this mean there were other organizations like Project 17 all over the world?

He only had a split second to register the thought before Isabel's arm shot out and Zak was forced to duck to avoid a missile flying at his head. It was a can of baked beans, one of several food cans stacked in the corner of the room. Provisions for hiding out here in the middle of nowhere.

"Hey!" Zak cried, narrowly avoiding the can. "We're not—" He got no further. She launched herself at him. He saw an expression of concentrated fury and determination on her face, then her shoulder hit his midriff and he was thrown onto his back, winded and gasping in pain.

He was still sprawling on the ground as she sprang up and raced off. He clambered to his feet. He glimpsed her silhouette in the glassless window for a moment, then she was gone.

Wow! She was fast!

But he knew he was faster.

Gritting his teeth, Zak sprinted after her, clearing the window frame in one smooth leap. She was running for a gap in the back wall of the fort. He focused, slipping easily back into the zone.

He saw Jackhammer appear at the edge of the broken section of wall. Hammer was a big guy – built like a rugby forward. He'd stop her, no problem.

Zak slowed as Hammer stepped into Isabel's path and spread his arms. Isabel jinked to the side as he snatched for her. Almost without breaking stride, she high-kicked him in the chest and rocketed past, leaving him staggering and gasping.

She was good.

Zak sped up again as she sprinted away from the fort.

"Nice try, Hammer," he said. "I'm on it."

Zak smiled to himself. Hammer was very competitive, he'd hate it that he'd failed where Zak was about to succeed.

Isabel was sprinting up the far slope of the valley now. Impressive. But Zak was on her heels before she'd gone even a quarter of the way.

Careful. She's a tricky one. He didn't fancy taking another hit from her. As he ran, he slipped the Taz out of his pocket. It looked like a slender black rubber torch, but it had a powerful battery and pincer-like electrodes at the business end. Touched against exposed skin it gave an electronic kick that could take down a grown man. The effect was only temporary, but it got the job done.

Isabel glanced over her shoulder. Her face registered surprise that he was so close.

Yeah, sorry about that. The super-speed thing gets them every time.

Zak was about to tag her with the Taz when she put on a spurt of speed that made him feel as if he was standing still.

What was *that*?

Stones and dust rained on him as she ran up the hillside. He only let himself be stunned for a moment. Then he went after her at top speed.

He concentrated hard, digging deeper into the zone. But still she was ahead of him. What was going on?

She vanished over the hilltop.

Zak came flying up to the ridge. The hill fell away into a steep ravine. From there he could see Isabel, already halfway down the far side, leaping and jumping from rock to rock like a mountain goat with a sugar rush. Zak had never seen anything like it.

Taking a deep breath he plunged after her. He had one thing clear in his mind: Isabel was no ordinary agent. She was easily as fast as him, and she had all his free-running skills.

Colonel Hunter hadn't warned them about this.

If Zak didn't pull something out of the bag pretty quickly, she'd get away.

And that would be a disaster. Not just for Project 17, but potentially for everyone on the planet.

CHAPTER **TWO**

LONDON. FORTRESS.
07:20. THREE DAYS EARLIER.

The main briefing room of the MI5 department called
Project 17 was a long, austere room thirty metres below
the bustling streets of London's Moorgate. A huge
plasma screen dominated one wall, faced by rows of
desks and chairs, almost like a classroom.

The lights were dimmed and a world map filled the
screen. Red spots pulsed on every continent. Colonel
Hunter, Project 17's chief, was speaking.

"Here you can see the places targeted by World Serpent agents," he told the five agents who were sitting watching the screen in attentive silence. "Terrorist atrocities or criminal activity linked to World Serpent have taken place in Melbourne, Hong Kong, Singapore, Beijing, and right across Asia. They have committed major robberies in Moscow and Kiev, Dubai and Cairo. Bombs have been detonated in Oslo, Berlin and Milan. A major attack was only just thwarted in Washington by FBI Assistant Director Reed and, as you know, Quicksilver and Wildcat were directly involved in Operation Silver Screen in Los Angeles." He clicked the remote and a slightly eerie symbol floated into view over the world map. The simple design of a ring formed of a red snake with its tail in its mouth. Within the circle of the snake was an illustration of the earth, showing the Pacific Ocean, with the Americas on the right and Japan, China and Russia on the left. Scribed across the ocean were the fiery letters WS.

World Serpent.

Zak knew that design well. He'd seen the snake eating its tail on the luxury super-yacht the *Ouroboros* off the coast of Paradise Cove in California. And he'd seen the whole logo on the computer of a World Serpent agent codenamed Raging Moon.

Since then he'd learned that an International Committee of Intelligence Departments had been hunting for information on the man who controlled World Serpent. A man known as Reaperman. The man who had killed Zak's parents only months after he had been born.

Zak and Cat's work in Hollywood had helped tighten the noose around Reaperman. Intel now pointed to him being a Greek billionaire businessman by the name of Achilles Rhea.

A series of surveillance pictures flashed up on the screen, showing dozens of men and women who had been linked to World Serpent. One picture dominated. A man aged around fifty-five, with a lined and weather-beaten face, a heavy, greying moustache, and a long mane of grey, swept-back hair. His eyes were deep-set, hooded and a strange dark-blue colour.

"This is Achilles Rhea," Colonel Hunter told them. "His mission plan for World Serpent is simple." There was a pause. "He wants to run the world and he doesn't care how much mayhem he causes along the way."

Zak vividly remembered World Serpent's Manifesto. He had seen it on a computer screen in the office of the one of Reaperman's captains. The chilling words had remained with him.

WORLD SERPENT MANIFESTO.
OUR AIMS AND PURPOSES.

Terror is a means to an end.

World Serpent will use whatever means necessary to fulfil its great destiny. As captains in my army, you each have your own orders and your own missions to accomplish. But understand that each of you is but a single cog in a great global machine.

The great warlords of antiquity performed marvellous deeds. Alexander the Great created one of the largest empires of the ancient world, Attila the Hun devastated the Roman Empire, Genghis Khan subdued the Asian continent, Ivan the Terrible controlled an empire of one and a half million square miles. But we will do more. We will bring down every government in the world. We will create mayhem and strife. We will create warfare and destruction on a scale that the old warlords never dreamed possible.

And from the anarchy and the lawlessness and the desperation that will engulf the world, we will rise and we will take power and there will be no one to stop us. Our mission has only just begun.

Reaperman

"So, he's crazy, right?" asked Jackhammer, a big, beefy agent with gelled brown hair and narrow eyes.

"Crazy like a rabid dog," said Wildcat, turning her large eyes on him. Cat's white hair stood up in spikes and her nails were painted black. The only Goth secret agent in the world, Zak had always thought.

"But can he actually do it, Control?" Switchblade asked the Colonel.

Zak had worked with Switch several times in the past. The tall, muscular sixteen-year-old had short, light brown hair and piercing blue eyes. He was a phenomenal gymnast and expert in Krav Maga and Wing Chun, as well as several other martial arts. A good guy to have your back in a crisis, as Zak knew all too well.

"That's the big question," said Colonel Hunter. "He has the money to fund his operations, we know that for certain. And we also know he was in the running to buy the device called Burning Sky."

Burning Sky. A small electro-magnetic pulse device with the capacity to take out all the electronics in a city in one go. Zak had been part of the team that destroyed the weapon, but he still sometimes woke up in a sweat at the thought of what could have happened if Burning Sky had detonated over London. He could hardly imagine the chaos that would have caused. No computers. No air traffic control to guide aeroplanes safely. No traffic signals. No hospitals. No police. Nothing. Just utter chaos and death on a vast scale.

"But that weapon doesn't exist any more, does it?" asked Moonbeam, a small girl with large green eyes and long red hair framing her pale, freckled face.

"It doesn't," agreed the Colonel. "But there are rumours that World Serpent has been working on something even more dangerous."

"Any idea what that would be, Control?" asked Jackhammer.

"Is it a WMD?" asked Cat.

Zak knew what that stood for. Weapon of Mass Destruction. A way to kill the largest number of people as possible at one time.

"We should assume it is," said Colonel Hunter. "It could take the form of a bomb or a virulent toxin. Or a poison like the one they tried to introduce into the Los Angeles water system." He lifted his hand, his fingers touching as though he were holding something very small. "Or imagine a tiny phial of some lethal virus," he said. "Ebola or Hepatitis B or Hantavirus or Dengue Fever. Imagine this phial being smashed in an international airport – New York or Heathrow or Hong Kong." He dropped his hand. "I don't need to spell out the effects."

No, he didn't. Millions of people could be infected within days. Hundreds of thousands would die.

"So what's the plan, Control?" asked Switch.

Colonel Hunter glanced briefly at Zak before speaking. "For the past two and a half years an undercover MI5 agent codenamed Slingshot has been working in Greece and on the Greek Islands of the Aegean and Ionian Seas," he told them. "Achilles Rhea is a known criminal he has been keeping an eye on. When he was informed that Achilles Rhea was our main suspect, he was sent *here.*" The screen changed to show a satellite image of a teardrop-shaped island.

"This is Panos, one of the Ionian Islands off the west coast of Greece. Slingshot's brief is to get as close as he can to Rhea's organization and find out about World Serpent's immediate plans." He turned away from the screen and pressed the remote to bring the ceiling lights up.

"The five of you are to join Operation Icarus," Colonel Hunter said. "Part of your task is to form back-up for Slingshot as and when he needs it."

"How do we make contact, Control?" asked Moonbeam.

"You don't," said the Colonel. "Slingshot will contact you when he thinks it's safe. Under no circumstances are you to try and seek him out. If he's done his job properly and he's close to Rhea, any attempt to contact him could be fatal. Passcodes have been arranged so you'll know each other. Slingshot will ask the question: 'Why did Icarus fall?'. The counter is: 'Because he flew too near the sun.' Memorize these call-signs. You'll need them."

"So, we sit around waiting for him to get in touch?" asked Hammer, not sounding impressed. Hammer was a punch-first-and-say-hi-later kind of a guy.

"No, you do not," the Colonel said sharply. "You will have plenty to do. Your operational remit will be downloaded to your Mobs shortly."

"Can you give us any more information about Slingshot, Control?" asked Zak. "Anything that might help?"

His eyes met Colonel Hunter's steely grey gaze. They both knew why he had asked that particular question.

MI5 Undercover Agent Slingshot was Zak's older brother Jason.

Up until a few months ago Zak had known absolutely nothing about his family. All he'd been told was that he had been found in a holdall on the steps of St Thomas's Hospital as a baby. He'd been placed in several foster homes, but hadn't settled in any of them. As a small child he'd been a loner, happy in his own company, and not great at mixing with others. As he'd got older he'd taken to long-distance running, and by the time he was ten, he was into free-running as well, and getting very good at it. That was about the time he was placed in the children's home, Robert Wyatt House.

His first encounter with Project 17 had been a total and horrifying accident. A pal of his at the home, a part-time pickpocket called Spizz, had been murdered, and the events that followed had put Zak in real danger and taken him to places he had never known existed.

Like Fortress, a network of rooms and offices thirty metres under London; the headquarters of a secret department of British Intelligence called Project 17 – a specialist group of agents, all of whom were in their teens.

That was when Zak found out that his ability to run fast was more extraordinary than he had ever suspected. And that was when he had been invited to join Colonel Hunter's team.

If that wasn't enough to fry his brain, the real story of his past also started to come out. His mother had been an MI5 field agent, and she'd been on a mission with his father when a terrorist called Reaperman had blown their aeroplane out of the sky over Canada. Zak had been three months old and the powers that be had decided it was safer for him to vanish into the social services system. Reaperman was notorious for wiping out entire families of people he saw as his enemies.

The next revelation to rock Zak's world had been the fact that he had an older brother. Jason had been eight when their parents were killed. He had been adopted and given a new life. But he'd learned that his mother had been in MI5, and at the unusually young age of eighteen, he too had been recruited into the British Secret Services. Codename Slingshot. Now he was in deep cover. Uncontactable.

Zak had only been given this last piece of the jigsaw a few weeks ago. He was desperate to know more, but Colonel Hunter dished out information in small doses as and when he thought it was appropriate to do so. Zak did his best not to let this drive him crazy, but it was really hard to know he had a brother alive somewhere in the world, and to know nothing else about him – apart from a codename and the knowledge that he had chosen the same career path as Zak.

"You have all the intel you need for the moment, Quicksilver," Colonel Hunter said. He gave Zak a slight nod. "Slingshot will make himself known to you at the right time."

Zak knew intel was handed out on a "need to know" basis – and the Colonel had made it very clear that for the time being he knew all he needed to know. He understood the Colonel's reasons for holding back, but there were times when Zak was amazed his brain didn't explode under the pressure.

"The back story for your trip to Panos is that Moonbeam's father has funded an adventure holiday for her and a few friends as a reward for passing her school examinations," continued the Colonel. "You will be flying to Panos in five days' time. A villa has been hired for you, and you will take the necessary equipment for camping out. Slingshot is the agent in charge."

"Why the delay, Control?" Wildcat asked.

"Panos is a mountainous island," said the Colonel. "I want you to undergo a hardcore refresher course for a few days in that kind of terrain. You're booked on a flight out of Heathrow at eleven-twenty this morning. By seventeen-thirty-five local time, you will be landing at Heraklion Airport in Crete. You will be met and taken to Field Station Zeus, where you will stay for three full days of training. From there you will fly direct to Panos. I don't need to tell you how important this mission is, agents." The Colonel walked to the door and opened it. "Dismissed," he said. "And remember – be smart, be safe."

Zak hung back as the others trooped out, murmuring excitedly under their breath.

"Control . . .?" he began.

"No 'buts' this time, agent," said the Colonel. "Remember everything I told you, and hang in there. Hopefully, all your questions will be answered soon."

And as frustrating as it was, Zak had to be content with that.

FIELD STATION ZEUS, MOUNT IDA, CRETE. TWO DAYS AFTER THE FORTRESS BRIEFING.

"You realize that if you fall, the rest of us are going down with you?" Cat called to Hammer as he hung precariously from a ridge three metres above her head.

"No one's going to fall," Hammer shouted down.

"Famous last words," muttered Zak.

Moonbeam grinned. "If he does, I bet he leaves a Hammer-shaped hole in the ground like in a cartoon."

"Less chat, guys," Switch called from the top of the ridge. He was standing on the brink with his legs planted firmly apart, both hands on the rope that connected him to Hammer. The rope snaked down to the narrow ledge where the other three agents were huddled, waiting their turn to make the tricky climb.

It was early in the morning of their second day of training. Mount Ida was a huge barren chunk of rock against the blue sky; impressive rather than attractive. Above 2,000 metres, there were no trees, no plants and no water. Just trekking up to that height from base camp at Zeus was exhausting enough, but their guide had them go to Grade Two scrambling on their first outing. Grade Two meant they were all roped together and then taken away from the easy tourist routes up to the summit. Grade Two meant steep ridges and gullies; it meant clinging on with your fingertips while you scrabbled around for a foothold.

It meant that if one of you fell, especially a chunky guy like Jackhammer, the rest of you would follow him down to the bone-cracking rocks fifty metres below.

Zak didn't feel comfortable on the ledge. The big mountaineering boots were cumbersome and heavy, and the rucksack weighed down on his shoulders, loaded with the basic necessities their instructor Stavros had insisted they all bring along. A map, a compass – even though their Mobs all had built-in GPS apps – spare sunglasses and sun cream, extra food, extra water and extra clothes. A torch, a first aid kit, a magnesium stick and a tin called Canned Heat for starting a fire. A knife. A thermal sleeping bag in case they got lost and had to spend the night up there.

Hammer hauled himself over the top of the ridge and Wildcat began to climb. She was about a third of the way up when the emergency signal went off on Switchblade's Mob.

Everyone stopped while he took his Mob out and checked the screen.

"Okay," he said. "We're done, for now. That was Fortress. Control needs to vid-link us ASAP. We're going back down."

Field Station Zeus was a stone and wood hut clinging to the lower slope of the mountain. Its windows looked out over the foothills and valleys where small stony villages huddled among groves of trees. In the far distance, the sea was a pale shimmer and on a clear early morning the north coast of Africa was visible.

The five agents gathered in Cat and Moon's room while Switch opened the vid-link on the laptop.

Colonel Hunter's face appeared on the screen. "I've just had some significant intel from the BND in Germany." Zak wasn't sure what the letters stood for, but he knew the BND was German Intelligence. "I've been told that one of their agents has been embedded in Achilles Rhea's organization for some time now."

"They had an agent on the inside and they didn't tell us?" said Switch. "How did that happen?"

"Their agent codenamed Isabel had nothing to do with the search for Reaperman or World Serpent," Colonel Hunter explained. "She was looking into links Rhea was thought to have with international arms smuggling and people trafficking. She's a teenager, working as kitchen staff."

"The Germans have teenage agents?" said Wildcat.

"Apparently they do," the Colonel said briskly. "We need not concern ourselves with that at the moment. I've been told by my contacts at the BND that Isabel has some important new information concerning Reaperman. The details are sketchy at the moment, but with Slingshot's help Isabel has escaped Panos with this information."

"How did they even know about each other?" asked Zak.

"Field agents in deep cover are given very subtle international passwords and codes so they can recognize one another and provide help in an emergency," the Colonel explained. "I believe that is what must have happened."

"Way to go, Slingshot!" murmured Jackhammer.

"It's not all good news," said the Colonel. "Rhea knows that Isabel is on the loose with some damning evidence against him. He has sent out several search parties and I'm told all Isabel's usual routes home have been blocked."

"Can Slingshot help her again?" asked Moonbeam.

"Not without compromising his cover," said Colonel Hunter. "My contact in BND tells me that their field agents have a default safe house that they are told to go to in an emergency situation. As you are the closest trained team in the vicinity, I've agreed to send you in to pick her up."

"Where is she, Control?" asked Switch.

"She's in Morocco," Colonel Hunter said. "In the Atlas Mountains. Bug will send you the exact co-ordinates shortly."

"We're on it, Control," said Switch. "We'll start packing immediately."

"There's one potential problem," said Colonel Hunter. "Isabel ditched all her electronic devices in order to be sure she couldn't be tracked. She isn't in contact with her headquarters, and if she thinks you're one of Reaperman's teams, she'll run." The Colonel's voice lowered to a rumbling growl. "She's a fully-trained field agent. Don't underestimate her. Call as soon as you have her. We need that information. Fortress out."

Switchblade closed the laptop and stood up. "Well," he said. "You heard the man."

Zak packed as quickly as he could, excited at the thought of some real action. Agent Isabel had met Jason – maybe there'd be the chance for her to tell him something about his brother. Even what he looked like would be great!

One thing was for sure – training was over.

CHAPTER **THREE**

FORT JEBEL LEKST. MOROCCO.
REAL TIME.

Zak threw himself down the ravine in Isabel's wake. He still couldn't quite make sense of what was happening. She wasn't just fast, she was amazing!

The bottom of the ravine was strewn with rocks and boulders. Isabel didn't break stride; she vaulted over the bigger boulders and leaped sure-footed from the tops of the smaller ones, her arms out for balance, her feet never faltering.

It was like watching himself on video, Zak thought. How was she doing this? Was she the same as him? Did she have the adrenaline imbalance thing too?

That kind of question was going to have to wait. He needed to catch her first. She was across the floor of the ravine in seconds. She didn't even bother glancing back as she sped up the far side, kicking stones and dust as she went.

No you don't!

Zak launched himself at the steep hill, entirely focused. He ignored the pebbles and grit raining down on him. The ground was loose under his feet, making it hard to dig in. But his mind was razor-sharp, plotting the best way up the side of the ravine so that every step brought him closer to his target.

Agent Isabel was on the top of the ravine now, a black shape against the bright white of the early morning sky. He was only a few metres behind her when two things happened at once. Zak heard the familiar sound of a four-wheel drive from somewhere close by, and in the same instant Isabel threw herself to the ground.

For a moment Zak thought it must be Moonbeam in the ATV. But the engine didn't sound right – and it was coming from the wrong direction.

A burst of automatic weapon fire crackled through the air and bullets kicked up spurts of dust along the ridge. Definitely not Project 17. They never used guns.

There was a screech of tyres as a black ATV lurched into sight. Zak ducked behind a rock as an armed man jumped out of the vehicle and strode towards where Isabel was lying.

"Get up!" the gunman shouted at her, gesturing with the muzzle of his machine pistol. He was dressed in black. He spoke English but with a heavy Mediterranean accent.

"Get up now, or I will shoot you where you lie. Reaperman wants you alive, but he will not care if I have to wound you."

Isabel got to her feet, hands in the air.

Her voice was full of fear. *"Ich verstehe Sie nicht. Nicht schiessen!"*

She was speaking in German. He recognized it from school, although he had no idea what she had said. So Agent Isabel didn't speak any English. No one had told them *that*.

The man made beckoning motions with his gun. Isabel stared at him as if she didn't understand what he wanted.

"Get. In. The. Auto," the man said, speaking slow and loud.

She backed off as he approached her, and Zak was startled to see terror in her face. She was supposed to be a trained agent. What was German Intelligence thinking, letting a girl like that out into the field? Isabel gave a wail and threw her arms over her head as the man reached for her.

What happened next was so quick that Zak could hardly follow it. Isabel jumped to one side, hooking her foot behind the man's knee and striking him in the chest with a skilled martial arts punch. He lurched backwards. Her foot whipped his leg out from under him and he crashed onto his back.

She was on him in a flash, one knee in his stomach, both hands on his gun as she tried to wrench it out of his grasp. But he wasn't about to be disarmed so easily. With a snap of his arm, he smacked Isabel on the cheek with the butt of the gun. She was thrown sideways as the man heaved himself up and crashed down on top of her, the gun against her throat.

Zak was up and running almost before he realized he'd made the decision. As he stormed over the ridge, he glimpsed the driver of the ATV clambering out of the vehicle. The man was holding a pistol.

Zak's foot caught the first gunman squarely in the side of the head. With a grunt of pain, he rolled off Isabel, but both of them still had a tight grip on the gun.

Zak tucked into a roll as he saw the driver raise the pistol and fire. There was a loud crack and the zing of the bullet ricocheting off a stone.

A moment later, the air was full of automatic gunfire. Zak threw himself to the ground as a spray of bullets burned through the air. Isabel and the man were still wrestling for the gun as it fired wildly in all directions.

Zak heard a low groan. The driver dropped to his knees and then fell onto his face. A stray bullet must have caught him. There was a sudden silence. Zak sprang up and saw Isabel standing over the first man, his gun in her hand, dangling from its strap.

"*Dummkopf!*" she growled at him. There was a raw red patch at the side of his head and he wasn't moving.

Zak walked towards her, hands out in front of him to show he wasn't a threat or an enemy. She turned her head slowly and looked at him.

"*Sprecken sie* English?" he asked hesitantly. "*Ich bin ein froynd*, okay?" He mouthed the word carefully, one eye on the gun. "*Froynd.*" That was German for *friend* . . . sort of.

She gave him a puzzled look.

He really wished he'd paid more attention in German class.

He tried again. "*Ich bin* from British Intelligence."

"Your German is appalling," she said with hardly a trace of a German accent. "Please do not try speaking it again."

Zak realized his mouth was hanging half open. He closed it. "You speak English, then," he said.

She pointed the gun at him. "Who are you? Tell me quickly. There will be more of these *schütze* nearby. We have not much time."

"My codename is Quicksilver," Zak explained. "I'm part of a team sent by British Intelligence. We're here to bring you in safely."

She looked unconvinced and Zak saw with some alarm that her finger was straying towards the gun's trigger. "Why was a British team sent?" she asked. "Why not German?"

"We were the closest," he said, wondering if he had any hope of disarming her if things went bad. "We were training in Crete. You can use my Mob to call your people if you have a number. They'll confirm I'm telling the truth."

"You have a Mob on you?" she asked with sudden interest. "I have heard of them. I would like to see it, please."

Zak reached for the Mob in his breast pocket.

Their heads snapped round at the distant sound of a car engine.

"Get to cover," Isabel hissed, ducking and running for the ATV. He followed her, crouching beside her on the driver's side.

"We were stupid," he said. "Standing there like that on high ground. Anyone with binoculars could have seen us."

But Isabel didn't seem to be listening. She had brought her backpack round and she was digging through it frantically.

Zak listened. From the growling and the churning of wheels he guessed that at least two vehicles were coming. Not good. He was out of the Imp's contact range. He took out his Mob and pressed the emergency code. The message flashed instantly to Switch's Mob along with Zak's precise co-ordinates.

Agent in trouble. Back-up needed.

Isabel pulled a memory stick out of her backpack. "Take it," she said urgently. "It is what you came for. Get it back to your people. I will lead the *schütze* in the wrong direction."

"No!" said Zak. "Look, I saw how fast you are, but you can't outrun a car."

She gave him a fierce grin. "I will not be running." She shoved the memory stick into his hands, then, keeping her head low, she slid into the driver's seat of the ATV. "Now, go," she said. "I know what I am doing. They will not catch me."

"No," Zak insisted. "Back-up will be here soon. We should stick together."

"Does this back-up carry automatic machine guns?" Isabel asked.

"No," Zak admitted.

"Then my plan is best," she said. "I will head north – you go south. They will follow me." She nodded at the memory stick. "Take that information to the right people. It is important, okay?"

"I'm not leaving you," Zak said. "We don't do that."

She glanced over her shoulder. The approaching vehicles were not in sight yet, but the noise of their engines was getting rapidly louder. It could only be a matter of a few seconds.

"Have it your own way," she said in an exasperated voice. "Get in."

He climbed in next to her as she revved the engine. The ATV lurched forwards as she spun the wheel. Zak went to close the door a moment too late. He felt a hand shove him sideways. He toppled out of the moving vehicle and saw Isabel's arm reach out to slam the door.

A moment later the air was full of grit and gravel as she gunned the engine and the ATV sped off.

Gasping, he watched the vehicle accelerate away. But he had no time to sit there staring. The others were coming in fast. He scrambled to the side of the track and sprawled flat behind some rocks.

He stayed there until he heard one . . . two . . . three heavy vehicles go thundering past. Then he lifted his head to see the dust settling. He couldn't believe he'd let Isabel ditch him like that. He hoped she'd be okay.

He pushed the memory stick into his backpack and ran across the road. He pressed out a rapid message on his Mob as he went racing down the long slope of the ravine and back towards the fort.

I have the intel. Hold your position. I'm coming in.

He glanced briefly over his shoulder as he ran. He hoped he would see her again. There were a few questions he'd like her to answer. Like, how come she could outrun him?

*

FORTRESS.
LONDON TIME: 16:25.
TEN HOURS LATER.

The Project 17 team had taken the first available flight out of Marrakech-Menara Airport. They had been met at Heathrow by an official car and whisked to London in record time.

They were given half an hour for a shower and a change of clothes before assembling in the briefing room.

The lights were dimmed as they watched the video that had been downloaded from the memory stick Isabel had given Zak. Colonel Hunter was with them, sitting on the edge of a desk, arms folded, his eyes fixed on the screen.

Apart from the voices coming from the plasma screen, the room was completely silent.

The video had obviously been made using a hand-held camera. It was shaky and grainy and the sound quality was uneven.

It showed a large room – some kind of laboratory, Zak assumed, judging from the long metal tables, the electronic devices, snaking cables and blinking LED lights. Half a dozen people in white coats moved among the tables, adjusting dials and faders and tapping notes on tablet computers. Scientists or doctors for sure, Zak thought. The walls and the stooping ceiling of the room were formed of rough grey rock, as if the laboratory was in a cave.

A thin-faced man in small round glasses and with receding oiled-down hair squinted into the camera's lens.

"Nice-looking guy," murmured Jackhammer. "Face like a demented lizard."

"Quiet, please," murmured Colonel Hunter.

"Is this thing recording?" asked the man, peering into the camera. He had an eastern European accent but spoke perfect English.

"Yes, Dr Zoli," said a muffled voice. "You can carry on now."

"Excellent," said Dr Zoli, walking away from the camera and making a sweeping gesture with his arm. "We are in the main research and development facility of Base Hades," he explained. "Around me you can see some of the equipment we have been using to help perfect SWORD."

Zak watched the screen with absolute concentration. Isabel had risked her life to get this intel out into the world. What was coming? He didn't like the sound of

Base Hades – Hades was the word in Greek mythology for hell. And what was SWORD?

The camera panned to a square metal table on which stood an odd-looking device supported by a tripod. The device was a complicated mass of tubes and wires and metal projections. Zak thought it looked like a motorbike engine that had been turned inside out and given a few sci-fi additions. A circular metal tube protruded from one end, surrounded by coils of silvery wire. The device had a keypad attached at the other end and cables snaked down, connecting it to some kind of power source.

"This is the first prototype of SWORD," Dr Zoli continued. "The acronym SWORD comes from the name Sonic Wave Resonator Device – S. W. R. D." He smiled thinly. "A little conceit of my own, I fear. But the name SWORD is appropriate, I think. SWORD has been designed and perfected to be able to create and release a sonic resonation capable of destroying any object it is aimed at." He turned from the camera and spoke briefly to one of the white-coats. The man tapped some numbers into the keypad on the device while another of them placed a wine glass on a nearby pedestal.

"It has long been known that certain specific sonic frequencies can shatter glass," said Dr Zoli. "Allow me to demonstrate."

Zak noticed he was holding a kind of remote. He pressed a button and a soft humming came from SWORD. The humming rose steadily in pitch and volume. Dr Zoli pressed another button. The device shuddered and there was a high-pitched stab of sound and a brief flash of light. A nanosecond later, the wine glass shattered into a thousand pieces.

"As you can see," said the doctor, "it is quite effective. But the unique property of SWORD is that it can be programmed to affect a whole spectrum of different and quite specific elements. Everything that exists has its own resonance – all we have to do is find that resonance and tune SWORD into it. For instance, SWORD could be programmed to the specific resonance of steel or stone or wood, and used very efficiently to destroy them." An unpleasant, reptilian smile curled his lip. "Or it could be tuned to something even more interesting." He turned. "Bring him in now, please."

An odd shiver of unease ran down Zak's back, as though some instinct was warning him that bad things were about to happen.

The briefing room was tense and hyper-alert as they watched a man being brought into the room between two armed guards. The man seemed to be exhausted, his feet dragging, his face haggard, his clothes ragged and torn.

"Tie him to the chair," ordered Dr Zoli.

"Someone's really gone to town on that guy," murmured Jackhammer. "He's been beaten half to death."

The man was pushed into a metal chair and bound to it hand and foot. One of the white-coats began to tap out numbers on SWORD's keypad.

"As I explained," said Dr Zoli, "SWORD's resonator panels can be reset to target anything at all. In this particular experiment, we have set the co-ordinates to a very interesting frequency indeed. This man works for Russian Intelligence. He was caught snooping on us. He is about to learn the truth of what we have been working on. Unfortunately for him, he will not benefit from that knowledge."

A shiver went down Zak's spine. Agent Slingshot – Jason – could so easily get himself into the same danger. One slip, and his brother could be the next man in that chair.

Dr Zoli lifted the remote and pressed a button. SWORD started humming again.

"Oh, no," Zak heard Moonbeam whisper. "I don't want to see this."

"Steady, there," said Colonel Hunter.

The humming grew louder and higher, but it sounded different this time.

The camera focused on the man who was writhing now in his bonds.

Zak winced. He had a sick feeling in his stomach.

A flash of blue light and a quick blast of sound came from the end of SWORD. The man screamed, thrashing in his bonds, his eyes bulging.

Blood began to trickle from his ears and eyes and nose and mouth. He flung his head from side to side, spitting blood, his screaming filling the room. Then he gave a final shudder, his head fell forwards and his body went limp.

Blood dripped down his front. The humming faded.

One of the white-coats stepped forward and put a stethoscope to the man's chest. He turned to Dr Zoli and nodded, smiling.

Zak could hear murmurs of disgust and shock all around him.

"In this case," said Dr Zoli, "the frequency used was one that turns the human brain to jelly. This man's brain was reduced to liquid slime inside his skull."

CHAPTER **FOUR**

Zak stared at the screen in horror. He was doing his best not to throw up. It was almost impossible to get his head around it. When he'd signed up to Project 17, it had never dawned on him that he would be involved in something so monstrous and so utterly unbelievable. It was like a crazy movie plot! Except that what he'd just witnessed was real – horribly real.

Switchblade's voice came out of the gloom. He sounded as revolted as Zak felt.

"Turn it off, Control," he said. "I think we've seen enough."

"I second that," said Wildcat. "That was the most vile thing I've ever seen in my life."

"Keep calm, people," came Colonel Hunter's voice, and even he sounded appalled, although Zak knew he must have already watched the video. "There are a few minutes left. You need to see it all."

We really don't, thought Zak. Watching that poor guy's brain being turned to mush was enough, surely?

Dr Zoli led the camera out of the laboratory cave and along a rocky tunnel lit by harsh halogen strips. A mesh steel floor echoed and rang under his feet. They came to a steel door with a round window in it.

Dr Zoli opened the door and the camera moved forwards into a vast cavern with a high domed metal roof. A huge version of the SWORD device dominated the floor, squatting on three thick metal legs, towering up twice Dr Zoli's height. Thick cables ran from it. LED lights flickered and pulsed.

"This is the first full-sized version of SWORD," Dr Zoli explained proudly. "It has been designed to bounce its sonic wave beam off a satellite in orbit around the earth." He smiled into the camera. "As you can imagine, this gives us the advantage of being able to aim at targets a very great distance away. The beam will be quite narrow as it strikes the satellite, but by the time it returns to the planet's surface, it has been calculated that it would affect an area up to ten kilometres in diameter." He rubbed his hands together. "Big enough, in fact, to take out an entire city. Imagine, in a few world-changing moments, we could literally liquidate several million people."

Zak could feel the tension in the room now. He could hardly breathe because of it. He'd confronted terrorists before, but he'd never had to deal with anything on this scale. Reaperman was planning to kill an entire city full of people in just a few sickening seconds. He couldn't quite grasp it.

"A test firing of SWORD is planned in a few days' time," said Dr Zoli. "If it is successful, more of the devices will be constructed and hidden in other parts of the world." He spread his arms, his face triumphant. "With such devices, World Serpent will control the entire planet! Reaperman has already chosen the first target. In a matter of days, SWORD will strike London."

The video ended and grainy grey hail filled the screen.

Colonel Hunter shut the plasma screen down and turned up the lights.

Zak could see his own emotions mirrored in the faces around him. Profound shock. Disgust. Alarm. And something like disbelief, despite what they had seen happen to the Russian agent.

"You're all booked on a flight out of Heathrow tomorrow morning," Colonel Hunter told them. "You will arrive at Panos International Airport at thirteen-fifteen local time. A car will be waiting to take you to your villa. Bug will download all the specifics of Operation Icarus to your Mobs." His voice took on a sharp edge. "But your mission brief is no longer simply to act as back-up to Slingshot – you will now be directly involved in the operation to prevent the SWORD device from killing millions of innocent people."

"Do you think SWORD can really do that much damage?" asked Switchblade.

"We have to assume it can," said the Colonel. "It has to be found and destroyed, and the people behind it have to be neutralized. That's all. Get something to eat and have an early night. You'll be woken at zero-five-hundred hours for the journey to Heathrow Airport."

"Why isn't an international task force being sent in?" asked Jackhammer. "We know where Reaperman is; we know what he's planning to do – why not go in heavy and finish this in one hit?"

"We still have limited intel about Reaperman's capabilities," said Colonel Hunter. "We believe he has constructed an elaborate underground complex, but we have no idea how large it is, or how well protected. We have to assume that any large force approaching the island would be detected in advance."

"Meaning they could walk straight into SWORD," added Switch. He grimaced. "Nasty."

"Very nasty indeed," said Colonel Hunter. "And remember, it's not just the device itself that we need to take out. We have to secure Reaperman and his team. If an assault force was held back only long enough for the scientists behind SWORD to escape the island, we'd be back to square one."

"You mean they'd set up somewhere else and start all over," said Moon. "Yes, I get it."

"There's an old saying," the Colonel said. "Softly, softly, catch the monkey. We need to go in soft and stealthy. If we go in hard and heavy, the monkey might escape." He stood up, his grey eyes glinting. "This is going to be the most important mission any of you has ever undertaken. Make me proud, agents. Dismissed."

Zak didn't feel much like talking on the flight to Panos. His fellow agents were just as subdued. They sat on the aeroplane, caught up in their own thoughts, checking the info Bug had downloaded to their Mobs. Staring out of the windows. Wondering what was coming.

Zak couldn't shake the image of that poor Russian guy with the blood coming out of his eyes and nose and ears and mouth. But what was even worse was remembering the expression of pleasure on the face of that creepy doctor. He gave Zak the shudders.

Just put me in a room with him for a couple of minutes. I'll wipe that smile off his face.

And then thoughts of his brother would come into his mind. Agent Slingshot. With every moment, they were getting closer. Tomorrow – or the day after – the two of them might finally get to meet. How amazing would that be?

Zak leaned back in his seat, gazing out of the window as he imagined Agents Quicksilver and Slingshot working together to capture Reaperman and to avenge the deaths of their parents at last.

The sun was blazing in a clear blue sky as the five Project 17 agents came out of Panos Airport and bundled into the back of the seven-seat MPV that was waiting for them in the forecourt.

The driver helped them load their bags and then they were off, driving along dusty roads lined with palm trees and white stucco buildings with red-tiled roofs. The car climbed out of the town and up through a sun-baked brown landscape of scrubby trees and bare hills. The heat shimmered on the tarmac and glinted on the many small roadside shrines. Zak was glad of the air-conditioning in the vehicle. The temperature gauge on the dashboard showed 33°C outside.

Switch had a map of Panos across his knees, and was examining it carefully as they bumped along. Wildcat was on her Mob, playing one of her mind-shredding logic games. Moonbeam was practising her Greek on the driver. Jackhammer was telling Zak about a mission he'd been on in Finland – something about wild chases across the snow on skis – but Zak wasn't really listening.

He wondered what Jason was doing right now. Where was he on the island? How soon would he make contact? Would they get along straight away or would it be weird for a while? Would Jason even remember him? There had only been three months between him being born and the family being ripped apart by Reaperman.

Zak was jolted suddenly out of his thoughts by the spectacular landscape. They had come out of the hills and the road was cutting its way across the steep brown flanks of mountains. To one side, the rugged and rubbled mountainside reared over them; to the other, beyond a narrow steel barrier, the island dropped away for hundreds of metres into the sparkling blue Ionian Sea.

The road zigzagged as it followed the contours of the mountains, sometimes hanging over a cliff edge with only a few centimetres of gravel between them and the fall, sometimes hugging deep under a frowning rock face that looked as though it might come down on them at any moment.

And as they drove, Moonbeam translated tales that the driver was telling – tales of cars plummeting over the edge, of high-speed crashes, of rockfalls and of the road being made as slippery as glass by heavy rainfall.

"This is not a safe place," Moon translated as the driver spoke. "For thousands of years people have come here and died on these mountains. Now, the roadside shrines show where cars have driven off the road. Every shrine marks a death. Be very careful, my friends – death lurks everywhere on this island. It was named after the god Pan. Your English word 'panic' has the same root." The driver laughed before continuing. "They say that if you hear the sound of Pan's pipes, they will lead you to your death." He laughed again. "They say many things. Do I believe?" He shrugged, steering the car at breakneck speed round a tight curve. "Who knows? But it is good to be wary, my friends. Death takes many forms on Panos. Be wary of it."

Oh, we will, thought Zak. Don't worry about that. We'll be *very* wary.

The villa was perched on a high hilltop among tree-covered slopes that led down to the sea. There were no other buildings nearby and the place could only be approached along a narrow, winding track between groves of olive trees.

As Zak heaved his bag out of the car and gazed up at the two-storey building with its white walls and orange roof tiles, he couldn't help wishing for a moment that they really had come here for an adventure holiday. Switch paid the driver and the MPV vanished among the olive trees in a cloud of brown dust.

Wildcat had the key, and Zak's faint hopes that Jason would be waiting for them inside were dashed as they entered the delightfully cool interior of the villa and found it unoccupied.

There was a welcome folder on the breakfast bar in the kitchen.

"There are three bedrooms," Cat read. "And there are some bikes in the garage that we can use when we want to go to the local town. Apparently it's about a ten-minute ride away. There's a map."

"And there's food and drink in here," said Jackhammer, opening the fridge. "Excellent."

"And a private swimming pool out the back," said Moon, opening a set of French windows that led to a veranda with a long wooden table shaded by a huge umbrella. The oval pool was at the foot of a set of stone steps, the clear water shining in the sunlight.

"Cat and Moon can share a bedroom," said Switch. "I'll draw straws with Silver and Hammer for who gets a room to themselves. Cat? Find a socket and plug in – I want to let Control know we're here."

A few minutes later they were huddled around a low table in the main living room as Cat opened a vid-link to Fortress.

"Everything's on target, Control," Switch reported as Colonel Hunter's face appeared on the screen. "No sign of Slingshot yet."

"Agent Slingshot has been in touch with us," said the Colonel. "He is employed on the island. He's been told to report four times daily with updates on the situation. If there's anything relevant, Bug will let you know. Do you know your first task?"

"We're taking a boat trip round the island tomorrow morning," said Switch. "Bug sent us all the details. Achilles Rhea has his set-up in a place called Kharkhinos

Cove. We're to ask the tour guide to take us there so we can do some snorkelling and scope the place out."

"Report back on your return," said the Colonel. "Fortress out."

Switch closed the laptop. "Okay, guys," he said. "Let's get settled in. Hammer, you're always hungry, so you can be in charge of food. Cat and Moon, scope the place out for bugs and trackers, just in case. Silver, I want you to do a tour of the perimeter. Check for anything suspicious. That's it. The real work starts at zero-seven-hundred."

CHAPTER **FIVE**

PANOS.
11:35, LOCAL TIME.

The *Agia Kiriaki* chugged slowly along the rugged coastline of Panos, heading south towards Kharkhinos Cove.

Zak and his fellow agents sat along the sides of the boat, under a canvas awning. They were wearing swimming gear and they'd already been in the sea twice with flippers and snorkels, exploring reefs while silvery fish darted away through the clear water.

Their guide was at the tiller, steering the boat with small expert moves as he talked to them. Zak had been quite surprised to find that the young man who ran the tours was English. His name was Jamie, he told them, and he'd only recently come to Panos, after some time working on other islands in the Ionian Sea. He was tall, well-muscled and handsome, and he seemed to know everything there was to know about the coastal waters and the history of the island.

As far as Jamie knew, they were a group of English teenagers on a holiday funded by a rich parent. They were careful not to give him any reason to think otherwise. They had no idea how far Reaperman's influence reached on the island – they couldn't risk letting something slip that might get back to him. Even Jamie might be a potential informant.

Softly, softly, catch the monkey. Right now, Operation Icarus was all about deception and stealth.

Jamie explained that the boat was called a *caique* – a traditional wooden-hulled fishing boat, gaff-rigged but converted for tourists and powered now by a modern diesel engine.

Zak had enjoyed the trip so far, and again he found himself wishing they had nothing more important to do here than search the reefs for octopus and starfish. But this boat trip had been planned to bring them as close to Achilles Rhea's lair as possible so they could scope the place out and get a sense of what they would be dealing with.

They rounded another green shoulder of land and Jamie pointed ahead.

"You can see Kharkhinos Cove now," he said. "It's that narrow inlet between the headlands. Now, I know you asked me to bring you here, but there's something I need to tell you before we go in." He grinned. "The local gossip is that the guy who owns the land on the northern side of this inlet is a gangster." He chuckled, as though he found the idea comical or absurd. "He built a villa, but apparently he used to spend most of his time on his luxury yacht. It even had a helicopter pad, would you believe? I mean, we're talking super-rich here."

Zak had no problem believing him. He'd encountered that yacht before. It was called the *Ouroboros*. He'd seen it first in a marina in Montevisto, and then it had turned up again off Paradise Cove in Los Angeles.

It was the super-yacht *Ouroboros* that had led them here. The yacht itself had been impounded by the FBI when the World Serpent agent known as Raging Moon had been brought down, but Bug had done some internet detective work and he'd traced the name of the owner. Achilles Rhea – AKA Reaperman.

"Apparently Mr Rhea sold the yacht a while back," Jamie continued. "He has a new one now. Smaller, but still pretty impressive. If he's at home, you'll see it moored in the inlet alongside a big black freighter."

"What does he need a freighter for?" asked Zak.

"Export and import, so I'm told," said Jamie. "He has a legit business in the islands, but the rumour is that he smuggles guns and drugs and even people." He grinned. "I don't know if any of this is true, of course, and the only reason I'm telling you about it is that sometimes Mr Rhea can be a bit funny about people coming into the cove."

"What kind of funny?" asked Wildcat.

"He doesn't like it," said Jamie. "He acts as if he owns the whole cove, but he doesn't – just the northern side. He even tried running a chain across the mouth of the inlet when he first bought his piece of land. And he started building a big landing dock, before the authorities put a stop to it. You can still see the steel girders he put up. They're rusty now and the whole project was abandoned."

"So, is he going to get stroppy with us?" asked Jackhammer.

"That's very unlikely,' said Jamie. "If I thought that, I wouldn't have brought you here. But I have heard tell of boats being chased off by Mr Rhea's employees." He shrugged. "Mr Rhea employs some pretty unsavoury characters, but there's nothing for you to worry about. I've been here before, and I've never had any trouble. It'll be fine. But once you're in the water, just remember to be smart and to keep yourselves safe."

A thrill like electricity zapped through Zak at Jamie's final words. He stared at him hard. *Be smart, be safe.* That was what Colonel Hunter always told them when they were heading off for a mission. Did MI5 agents use the same phrase?

He swallowed a sudden lump in his throat. Jamie was English. He had only recently come to Panos. He knew the islands well . . . the way he would if he'd been scoping them out as an undercover agent for the past two years.

Jason?

Zak looked into Jamie's face, trying to see some kind of family resemblance. Was he Slingshot? Or was it just a coincidence?

Should he say something, make himself known? But if Jamie was Jason, he'd already know what was going on. If Agent Slingshot had decided not to reveal himself to them, he must have good reason. Frustrating and maddening as it was, Zak decided to say nothing. Be patient. As Colonel Hunter had told him, he'd find out everything he wanted to know when the time was right.

Zak tore his eyes away from Jamie. His heart was hammering wildly in his chest and he felt a little light-headed at the thought that he might be only a few metres away from his long-lost brother.

Calm down. Focus. Think of the mission.

All the while Jamie had been speaking, the *Agia Kiriaki* had been chugging gradually closer to the inlet.

They were at the mouth of Kharkhinos Cove now. Zak and the others moved to the prow to get a better look. The finger of dark blue water stretched back for about a kilometre, the sides of the inlet rising up steeply on either side. The high slopes were blanketed in trees through which hunks of rugged white rock showed like bleached bones. High on the northern side of the cove, Zak spotted the white walls and orange roofs of a large villa. Achilles Rhea's home, he assumed. There were no other visible buildings and the whole cove had a wild and remote look about it.

Moored close under the northern flank of the cove was a large black ship – obviously the freighter Jamie had told them about. And tucked in under the tall hull of the freighter was a luxury motor yacht. It was smaller than the *Ouroboros*, as Jamie had said, and this one didn't have a helipad, but even at a glance Zak could see that it was the kind of boat that only the world's richest people could afford.

As the *Agia Kiriaki* turned into the inlet, Switch pointed. "There's the remains of the dock," he said. Jutting from a low-lying shoulder of rock just above the water, Zak saw rust-brown steel girders that formed a half-finished grid shape. More girders rose vertically from the sea, their lower surfaces green with algae and seaweed.

Zak shaded his eyes against the sunlight that sparkled on the rippling water. He made out the word *Cerberus* on the side of the yacht.

"I know that name," he said, frowning. "Where have I heard it before?"

"Cerberus is the name of the three-headed dog who guards the gates of hell in Greek mythology," said Wildcat. She raised an eyebrow. "Cute! Or possibly not."

"Mr Rhea is really into Greek myths, isn't he?" said Moon. "His headquarters is called Base Hades, his yacht is called Cerberus. I'm surprised his alias isn't Pluto, Lord of the Underworld."

"He probably avoided it because of the dog in the old Mickey Mouse cartoons," said Switch. "Still, it means we're in the right place." He lowered his voice. Jamie was at the far end of the boat, still at the tiller, but Switch was determined to be cautious. "Remember, all of you – act naturally," he said under his breath. "We're just a bunch of goofy kids on holiday. If anything goes down, don't react like Project 17 agents. Got me?"

There was a general murmur of agreement.

The low throb of the *Agia Kiriaki*'s engine died and they heard the rattle of chains for the stern of the boat. Jamie was letting down the anchor.

"Okay, people," he called. "You know where the snorkelling gear is kept – go and enjoy yourselves."

Zak lay face-down on the smooth surface, kicking himself along and gazing into what he guessed was about four or five metres of crystal-clear water. The sea bed was an alien landscape of sand, algae-covered rocks and waving green fronds. Small silver and black fish darted this way and that, their shadows rippling along the bottom.

Zak and Moon were carrying small waterproof cameras. Their brief was to photograph anything unusual.

The water was warm and still. Turning his head from side to side, his field of vision limited by the sides of the facemask, Zak could see the dark shapes of his friends fanning out on either side. Behind him, the hull of the *Agia Kiriaki* was a black wedge, the anchor chain snaking down.

Someone splashed closer and Zak saw Switch beckoning under the water. Switch swam off and he followed. The submerged shape of a boat came into view, lying among the rocks. Its engine was visible through the cracked-open hull, the metal still shining, the curled plastic and steel piping like the intestines of a dead animal.

Zak videoed the wreck as he floated above it. It couldn't have been down there long. There was no rust. No coating of algae. And the hull looked as if it had been ripped apart by some kind of impact. Zak's stomach knotted. He wondered whether the boat had belonged to that Russian guy. Dr Zoli had said he'd been caught snooping.

Zak moved away from the eerie wreck and headed for the rusty steel framework of the abandoned dock. The girders loomed suddenly out of the water. Beyond them Zak could see a wall of black rock where the steep hillside plunged under the sea. He swam closer, aiming his camera.

He saw Moon moving between the dark fingers of metal.

Suddenly, she veered off, her feet splashing as she headed closer to the fists and knuckles of rock. He followed. She was hanging in the water now, her arms reaching down as she pointed her camera at something Zak still couldn't quite make out.

He came up alongside her. There was a strange, smooth surface in among the rocks, lying at an angle, about three metres below the surface. There was the dull glint of metal. At first Zak thought it was just a sheet of steel that had fallen into the water and become lodged between the rocks. But then he saw that it was a hatch of some kind. An entrance.

Zak and Moon turned their heads to look at one another. Moon gave the thumbs up and Zak did the same. They had definitely found something. This had to be the underwater entrance to the hidden bunker Control had mentioned in the briefing.

An odd buzzing noise filled Zak's ears. It got louder, turning into a booming growl that made his ears ring. He realized that it was the sound of a motorboat approaching.

He and Moon swam away from the hatch. Zak shoved his camera into an inner pocket in his swimming trunks. He lifted his head and pushed his facemask up. A small motorboat was cutting a white wake through the water towards them.

Zak could see the heads of Hammer and Wildcat and Switch bobbing on the water a little way off. Switch waved a friendly hand at the motorboat.

Zak remembered the drill: kids on holiday.

The boat came to a stop and a young man with dark hair stood up. "You are trespassing," he called. He spoke in English, but with a Greek accent. "You will return to your boat and leave here immediately."

Switch swam towards him, the snorkel dangling around his neck, the mask up over his forehead.

"Are you sure?" he called up, treading water close by the side of the boat. "We were told it was okay to be here."

"You were wrongly informed," said the young man. "This cove is private property."

Wildcat swam to Switch's side. "We're really sorry," she called to the man. "We weren't doing any harm."

"Nevertheless, you must leave now."

Hammer had swum close to the boat as well.

"Who owns it?" he called.

"That is none of your business," replied the young man. He pointed back to the *Agia Kiriaki*. "Return to your boat and tell the captain we will not be so reasonable if he comes here again."

"Calm down, mate," said Hammer. "No need to get

your knickers in a twist. We were just having a bit of fun."

Zak and Moon swam over to the others.

"We should go," said Moon. "We don't want to cause any trouble."

"We're off now," Switch said to the man. His voice dripped with irony. "Thanks for being so hospitable."

The man glowered at him but said nothing.

Switch began to swim towards the *Agia Kiriaki*. Zak and the others followed. As he climbed up the boat's ladder, Zak saw that the dark-haired young man was still watching them.

Nice try, creep, he thought. But you were too late. I'm pretty sure we got what we came here for. That underwater hatch had to be a way into Reaperman's lair. Now they could report their discovery back to Colonel Hunter and measures could be set in motion to bring his plans crashing down around his ears.

WATERLOO STATION. LONDON.

A tall, shaggy-haired and bearded man made his way through the growing night towards the arches under

Waterloo Station. He was wearing a long black coat over a ruined old suit that had once had pinstripes. His shoes were held together with duck tape and string.

Zak would have recognized him in a moment. He knew him as Dodge.

Dodge lived in a construction of hardboard and plastic sheeting he called "The Mansion". A few other street people shared his dark arch, setting fires in an old metal barrel for warmth when the nights grew cold, their sad, meagre belongings gathered around them in bags and boxes.

Zak had known Dodge for almost three years, ever since he'd seen the tramp on Waterloo Bridge and offered him half of his sandwich. They'd become friends. Since then Dodge had been the one person Zak could go to with his worries and problems. Dodge was a great listener. He was the only person outside MI5 Zak had confided in when he'd been recruited into Project 17 and his life had changed forever.

Zak had never asked his friend about his former life or how he'd ended up living on the streets, but Dodge had let one piece of information slip. He'd spent eleven years as a soldier. Zak assumed that something must have gone horribly wrong for Dodge to end up sleeping rough.

As Dodge walked back, carrying a warm kebab he'd bought with money he'd begged in the station, some old instinct kicked in. He glanced over his shoulder. A black van was gliding along the road behind him. Tinted windows. Moving slowly.

Dodge pocketed the kebab and sped up a little.

The van tracked him as he turned a corner and moved into the narrow side street that led to the arches.

That was all the proof he needed. This dingy street led nowhere. He was being followed. He broke into a run, his coat-tails flying. The van accelerated, gears grinding as it swept past him and came to a screeching halt across his path. The side door rolled back and four men in black leaped out.

Dodge fought hard, but they were professionals and the unequal battle lasted only a couple of minutes. Reeling from a blow to his head, Dodge was thrown bodily into the van. The men piled in after him and the door was slammed.

"Go!" a voice shouted. The engine roared and the van sped off. Two of the men held Dodge down while a third one tightened plastic strips around his wrists and ankles.

CHAPTER SIX

PANOS.
LOCAL TIME: 20:23

Zak and the others were gathered around a table outside
a harbour-front restaurant in the town of Faunos. They
had come here because it was the biggest town in that
part of Panos and they were hoping to gather some
local intel on Achilles Rhea. Their bikes were lined up
along the side wall of the restaurant. A whole row of
restaurants stretched down the curve of the harbour,
each with tables set up outside under huge square

umbrellas. But they had chosen Kiki's restaurant in particular because Bug's intel had informed them that Rhea often dined here.

They'd been in contact with Fortress earlier that afternoon, downloading images of the hatch that Moon and Zak had videoed. The general opinion was that the underwater hatch must lead into Base Hades. How they would ever be able to get in through the hatch and infiltrate Reaperman's headquarters undetected was another matter. Colonel Hunter and his team back at Fortress were already working on that.

"Are you ready to order?" A tall young man stood at their table, smiling, a pad and pencil in his hands.

Zak looked up, surprised to hear yet another English voice on the island. The young man's face was tanned and his hair was spiked in a gelled spray.

"Another Brit?" asked Moon with a grin. "Are there any Greek people on Panos at all?"

"One or two," he replied with a laugh. "My name's Oliver, by the way."

They introduced themselves, using the aliases Bug had given them. Zak was Danny, Switch was Steve, Moon was Bethany, Cat was Emily and Hammer was Charlie. They fed him the cover story of Moon's rich parents and then ordered some food.

As their meal progressed and the sun set over the harbour, Oliver would often pop back to their table to see how they were getting on and to bring them fresh drinks.

The sky darkened and stars flickered in the sky. Lights went on in some of the boats moored close by and candles were lit on the tables of the restaurants lining the seafront. A man strolled past playing a mandolin. People came and went, laughing and chatting, carrying bags of souvenirs from the many local tourist shops. The restaurant gradually filled.

Oliver came and sat with them on his break. "If you're feeling adventurous," he told them, "there are some great walks in the hills." He pointed to a long strip of land covered with thick trees across the other side of the harbour. "There are some interesting ruins over there, as well as an old lighthouse," he said. "But my favourite walk takes you up over the hills towards Kharkhinos Cove. I know a great way that avoids the usual tourist tracks. You can have the countryside all to yourselves." He gave a quick description of the landmarks they should use to get across the hills to the cove. "There are some spectacular views," he continued. "Although you don't want to go too close to the private property on the north side."

Zak's ears had perked up at the mention of Kharkhinos Cove. "Why not?" he asked, working to sound casual.

"It's owned by a gentleman called Achilles Rhea," said Oliver. "A frequent customer of ours. A very interesting fellow. If you like that type."

"What type is that?" Cat asked.

Oliver leaned close. "Some people say he's a crook," he told them in a low voice. "I've heard stories of people getting beaten up by his men. But as long as you keep on this side of the wire fence he put up, you'll be okay. Avoid the heavies, and you won't have a problem."

"Do you really think he's a crook?" asked Switch.

Oliver shrugged. "It's possible," he said. "He comes here now and then. He's a good tipper, so what do I care?" He smiled and got up. "Back to the grindstone," he said. "Give me a shout when you're ready for dessert."

Zak watched Oliver move away among the crowded tables. An odd thought had struck him. He leaned towards Switch, speaking in a whisper.

"Do you think it was a coincidence that Oliver just told us how to get to Kharkhinos Cove?" he asked. At one point he'd thought that Jamie from the boat might be Slingshot, but he wasn't so sure now. Was Oliver a more likely choice – after all, posing as a waiter in Reaperman's favourite restaurant would give him plenty of opportunity to overhear private conversations.

Switch gave him a thoughtful look. "You think the local

info he fed us was a bit too useful to be a coincidence?" he murmured. He nodded. "I was wondering the same thing."

"Slingshot?" mouthed Moon. "Really? But we were told he was working for Rhea."

"He could be doing both," said Zak. "Working for Rhea in the day and waiting tables in the evening."

Cat leaned in close. "I can see family resemblances to Silver," she said under her breath. "Same colour eyes, for a start."

"And that loony sticky-up thing he's done with his hair," added Hammer. "That's just like Silver."

"I'm not convinced," muttered Switch. "But if it is Slingshot, he obviously doesn't want to make himself known yet."

"But we can still use his intel to get to Kharkhinos Cove by land," said Cat. "Shh. He's coming back."

"Try this calamari," said Hammer in a louder voice. "It's really great."

"Squid?" said Moon with a shudder. "I don't think so. When I feel the urge to eat deep-fried elastic bands, I'll let you know."

They were all laughing as Oliver arrived and leaned over the table. "Speak of the devil," he said softly, making a subtle gesture across the restaurant. "Don't be too obvious with the staring, please, but that man over there is Mr Rhea. I don't recognize the other two men with him." He dropped his voice even lower. "They're probably dodgy business partners of his, what do you think?" He smiled and slipped away.

Zak and the others had been too well trained in covert surveillance techniques to turn and stare at the man, but Moon was facing that side of the restaurant, and she took out her Mob. "Say cheese, guys," she said, clicking the camera on her Mob several times while the others leaned together for what they hoped would look like group photos.

A few moments later, Moon had sent the pictures to all of their Mobs. Zak checked the pictures out. He recognized Rhea immediately from the photographs he'd seen in Fortress. He looked a bit heavier and his moustache was greyer and thicker, but he would know that tanned and weather-beaten face anywhere. Zak felt a shudder of loathing and hatred as he looked at Rhea's picture. He had to fight the urge to turn and stare directly at him. This man had almost certainly given the order that had killed his parents. He was determined that Rhea would pay for what he'd done.

Achilles Rhea had two men with him. Casually dressed. Ordinary looking. Probably in their forties.

A brief message came through from Bug.

Got the pix. Checking the other two with all databases. Back to you ASAP.

Moon had obviously sent copies of the pictures to Fortress.

"I'd love to know what they're talking about over there," murmured Switch.

"Leave it to me," said Wildcat. She got up and edged through the tables, heading for the restaurant.

There were soft croaks from their Mobs. Bug was seriously into frogs and all of his ringtones were of exotic frog-calls. Zak checked his Mob.

"One of the men is English. Ben Grafton. Big London-based crime boss. Suspected of arms dealing and plenty of other bad stuff. Control says keep surveillance at arm's length. We think the other man is one of Grafton's enforcers."

So, Rhea was having dinner with a couple of big-time London crooks. That made it even more important to listen in on what they were saying.

Shortly after that Zak saw Wildcat making her way back to them. She passed Rhea's table, stumbling and almost toppling over the man Bug had told them was called Ben Grafton. Zak saw her apologize, smile and move on.

She sat down. "I slipped my Mob under the table by one of the legs," she said under her breath. "It's on record. I'll pick it up again when they leave."

"That was a risky thing to do," said Switch. "These aren't normal guys, Cat. They probably have hair triggers for anything out of the ordinary."

"Did you have a better plan for finding out what they're talking about?" asked Cat. "The whole point is that we look like a bunch of innocent kids. Even if they spot it, I'm just a ditzy English teenager who dropped a phone. We'll be fine."

"I hope so," said Switch. He took a long breath then nodded and smiled. "Okay, ditzy teenagers, who wants dessert? I'm having baklava. Let's eat slowly; we could be in for a long evening."

CHARING CROSS POLICE STATION. LONDON.

Dodge sat in the cell, his back against the wall, his feet up on the bench as he finished the plate of fish and chips that lay in his lap.

The men in black had dumped him in here without a word. Police officers had come and gone, making sure he was all right, but not answering his questions. In fact, they acted as though they couldn't hear him when he spoke. They brought him food and drink and one of them even handed him a newspaper to read. But that was all.

Dodge heard keys turning. The cell door opened.

Now what?

A tall straight-backed man entered the cell. He had grey eyes and grey hair. From his bearing, Dodge knew in an instant that he was military or ex-military. An officer, for sure.

Dodge watched the man as he closed the door behind him.

"Do you mind if I sit?" the man asked.

"Help yourself," Dodge replied warily.

The man sat at the far end of the bench. "Have you been treated well?" he asked.

"That depends on your attitude to kidnapping," Dodge replied.

"Ah, yes." The man frowned. "I wasn't in charge of the team that picked you up. I apologize for the . . . over-enthusiastic way it was carried out." He looked at Dodge. "I am Colonel Hunter. I believe you've heard of me, Sergeant Carter."

Dodge started at the use of his real name and rank.

"I haven't been a sergeant for eight years," he replied, keeping his voice level despite the questions and doubts that were crowding through his mind.

"I've been reading your file," said Colonel Hunter. "You had an exemplary record, Sergeant. Recruited into the SAS from university. Rising through the ranks at unusual speed. Highly trained in the use of explosives – especially marine explosives. You were a sergeant by the time you were in your mid-twenties. Leading your men on twenty-three covert missions in the Middle East. Awarded the Queen's Gallantry Medal for action in Afghanistan."

Dodge glowered at him. "Ancient history," he muttered.

"You were leading a covert-ops team when you were attacked by insurgents in overwhelming force," Colonel Hunter continued. "Everyone but you and one of your men were killed. Despite your own injuries, you carried your wounded comrade through fifteen miles of desert until you were picked up and flown to a military hospital in Turkey."

"I know all this," growled Dodge. "What of it?"

Colonel Hunter carried on as if Dodge hadn't spoken. "You were brought back to the UK to recover from your injuries, but you disappeared from the military hospital in Aldershot." The Colonel paused. "And that's where your file comes to a sudden stop," he said. "Special Air Services Sergeant Tony Carter effectively ceased to exist from that moment." He looked Dodge up and down. "Your file suggests you had some kind of emotional or mental breakdown. Judging by the life choices you made, I'd say that was a good assessment."

"I didn't go crazy, if that's what you think," said Dodge. "I decided I'd had enough, that's all. Enough death and disaster for one lifetime. Do you blame me?"

"Not at all," said the Colonel. "But your services are required again, Sergeant."

Dodge snorted. "Forget it," he said.

Colonel Hunter looked at him for a few moments, as though weighing him up. "Project 17 has a use for your particular expertise," he said at last. "Your friend Zak Archer is on an extremely dangerous mission, Sergeant Carter. He needs you."

Dodge's eyes widened.

A heavy silence filled the small cell.

Dodge stared into Colonel Hunter's eyes. For a long time, the two men looked steadily at one another. Unblinking. Unspeaking.

*

It was a warm and starry night as Zak and his fellow agents gathered around the long table on the veranda above the swimming pool back at the villa. The pool was a bright, luminous blue and more spotlights picked out individual olive trees in the grounds. Beyond the hills, Zak couldn't distinguish where the sea ended and the sky began. An occasional bat swooped past, a black fleck skimming low across the sky.

Wildcat's Mob lay on the table, plugged into the laptop. They were listening to the conversation that had taken place at Achilles Rhea's table earlier that evening.

Cat's plan had been a total success. As far as they could tell, none of the men at the table had spotted the Mob lying on the floor next to their table, recording everything they said. Rhea and his guests had left after less than an hour and Cat had retrieved her Mob on their way to their bikes for the winding ride home.

The conversation between the three men was in English. Zak assumed the two Londoners didn't speak any Greek.

A lot of the talk involved ordering expensive wine and food, and as the minutes ticked by, Zak learned nothing more interesting than the fact that a bottle of Château Margaux wine cost over eight hundred Euros. He was beginning to wonder if the whole exercise had been a waste of time.

But then Rhea said something that changed the whole conversation.

"The Awakening of Perses is scheduled for zero-six-hundred-hours Greek time in two days," Rhea said in his heavy accent.

"That's four in the morning, UK time, right?" said one of the other men.

"Correct," said Rhea. "I need you and your associates to be away from ground zero well before then. Can you do that?"

"No problem," said the other man. "We'll take a flight back to Heathrow tomorrow morning and get everyone out of range in plenty of time. We've seen all we needed to see here."

"And SWORD impressed you?" asked Rhea.

"The video of what it can do impressed me," replied the other man. "Have your people got that girl yet? The one who copied the video and skipped out with it?"

Zak knew he must mean Isabel.

"She was tracked to Morocco, but she slipped the net," said Rhea. "She cannot get to her home base. It is only a matter of time before she is dealt with."

"She hasn't managed to contact anyone who could be a problem for us?" asked the man.

"My sources say not," Rhea said.

"Your sources are pretty useless then," muttered Zak. All the same, he hoped Isabel would be able to stay clear of Reaperman's people.

"Fill your glasses, my friends," said Rhea. "Let's drink to the Awakening of Perses and the end of the world as we know it."

"And to the money that's to be made afterwards," said the other man.

"Money?" said Rhea. "You and your kind are welcome to the money, Mr Grafton. It's the power I want. And it's the power that SWORD will give me. The kind of power that no man has ever known before. Ultimate power."

The manic tone in Rhea's voice sent chills down Zak's spine.

There was the clink of glasses.

"He's potty, isn't he?" muttered Hammer. "Totally off his trolley."

"You can say that again," Cat added, shaking her head. "I know Control told us about World Serpent's plans – but to actually hear it out loud . . ." She shuddered. "It's almost unbelievable."

The conversation between the three men continued for a while, but nothing else of significance was said.

Switch stopped playback. A sub-screen on the laptop showed Colonel Hunter and Bug. The recording had been fed to them as Zak and the others had listened.

"In case anyone is wondering," said Bug, "Perses is a character from Greek mythology. He was one of the Titans – the god of destruction."

"More mythology," said Moon. "What is it with that guy?"

"He's a nut-job," said Hammer. "He's in need of a nice padded cell."

"He deserves a lot worse than that," muttered Zak.

"We can assume the Awakening of Perses is the codename for the attack on London," said the Colonel. "Now we have a deadline. By my calculations, that gives you approximately twenty-nine hours to complete your mission."

"Check that, Control," said Switch in a grim voice. "We're on it."

Zak was woken by Jackhammer shaking his shoulder. "Code Platinum," Hammer hissed. "Something's going on downstairs."

Zak sat up. Code Platinum meant trouble. Hammer padded to the door and opened it a crack. Zak rubbed his eyes and forced his mind into gear. Switch had attached sensors to the insides of all the doors into the villa. No one should have been able to get in without tripping alarms.

There was a sudden crash.

Hammer yanked the door open wide and rushed onto the landing.

Zak was hard on his heels. He heard Moon cry out. Moon and Cat had taken the bedroom on the ground floor. Switch came from the other first-floor bedroom, his hair tousled but his eyes sharp. He had a Taz in his hand.

Switch leaped down the stairs five at a time, with Hammer and Zak close behind. They saw Cat and Moon battling furiously in the living room with two black-clad men. Hammer slapped the light on. One of the men delivered a powerhouse kick to Cat's midriff and she was flung heavily against the wall.

Moon ducked a wildly swinging punch as the two men ran for the French windows that opened onto the veranda. Zak saw that one of them had something under his arm.

Zak raced after them, but the other man flung something that exploded in a cloud of thick black smoke right at his feet. He staggered, coughing and blinded. Someone collided with him and they both fell heavily.

Zak was vaguely aware of someone jumping over them.

A few moments later, he heard a car engine revving furiously. There was a squeal of rubber and the sound of a car moving rapidly away.

Moon helped Zak to his feet. Switch came back in through the French doors in a swirl of dark smoke, his hand over his nose and mouth.

Hammer got up, shaking his head from where he had struck the stone floor. He let out a stream of swearing as the five of them stumbled into the kitchen to get away from the smoke.

Cat got Hammer to sit at the table while she dabbed at the cut on his forehead with a wet cloth. Switch was leaning over the table, panting and grim-faced.

"Is there any chance in the world that was just a regular burglary?" he said.

"Not much," said Cat. "They must have disabled the sensors on the French windows – and that would have taken some pretty sophisticated kit."

"They took the laptop," added Moon. "They were in and out again in a few minutes."

Switch shook his head. "Stupid! Stupid! Stupid!" he

said. "I should have had someone on watch." He looked up. "We were caught off guard," he said. "That should never have happened."

"They won't find out anything from the laptop," said Moon. "Bug's Trojan horse will fry the motherboard as soon as they try to use it without the password."

"But that's not the point, is it?" said Zak. He was at the sink. He cupped water in his hand and splashed it over his face. The smoke was making his eyes smart, and his nose was still full of its bitter smell. He looked at Switch. "This means someone knows who we are, doesn't it?"

Switch nodded. "Our cover has been blown," he said. "Anyone got a Mob handy?"

Cat ran to her bedroom and came back with the small silvery smartphone in her hand. She was tapping it as she returned, but she handed it straight to Switch.

They sat around the table as Switch was put through to Colonel Hunter. Switch reported the incident, keeping his voice surprisingly calm under the circumstances. Zak knew that Switch must feel responsible for what had happened; he could see the anger and dismay in his face. Switch put the Mob on loudspeaker so they could all hear Colonel Hunter's response.

"This is a setback," he said, and his voice was also calm and controlled. "You were taken unawares, there's no denying that. We must assume the intruders were working for Reaperman."

"I think I know what might have happened," said Wildcat despondently. "Rhea or one of the others must have seen the Mob under their table at some point. Probably towards the end, or Rhea wouldn't have talked about the Awakening of Perses. I knew it was risky, but I also knew we needed a way to get that information. I'm sorry, Control – that's my fault."

"I don't get it," said Hammer. "If they saw the Mob, why not just stamp on it or take it away with them? Why leave it there like it was nothing?"

"If they'd done that we'd have been on the alert," said Switch. "My guess is that as soon as Rhea saw it, he realized it wasn't just some teenager's smartphone. He would have wanted to know exactly who we were and what we were up to."

"I was reckless, Control," said Cat. "This is entirely down to me. I acted without asking Switch."

"I'm not interested in apportioning blame," said the Colonel. "Learn and move on, Wildcat. Now then – Switchblade? What do you intend to do?"

Zak saw Switch's jaw set. "We need to get out of here," Switch said. "Those two were only here on an information gathering grab-and-run raid, but we have to assume Reaperman will send in a larger force once they realize the laptop isn't standard issue."

No kidding, thought Zak. He'll figure that out the moment the laptop goes *kablooie* when someone tries to open it. Project 17 laptops had a sequence of tiny touch-sensitive pads along the side. They had to be triggered in a specific sequence before the thing was opened, or it was bye-bye motherboard.

"Have you had any contact from Slingshot yet?" Colonel Hunter asked.

"Not officially," said Switch. "There was an English waiter at the restaurant who was very chatty. Could you send us a picture of Slingshot so we can confirm?"

"Negative," said the Colonel. "When Slingshot wants to make himself known, he will. For the time being, I need you to stick to the original game plan."

"There was another English man," said Zak. "He called himself Jamie. He ran the boat tour. I thought he might be Slingshot . . . but I'm not sure now." He looked at his colleagues. "It could be either of them . . ."

"Or neither," said Hammer.

"Agent Switchblade?" Colonel Hunter's voice cut across their speculation. "Get your people out of there and report when you've found a safe haven. Fortress out."

Switch tossed the Mob back to Cat. "You heard Control," he said. "Get your stuff together – we're moving out."

Zak ran upstairs and began to shove his belongings into his holdall.

Reaperman was on to them – things were hotting up.

CHAPTER **SEVEN**

The sun was still hidden behind the hills, but dawn was breaking and the eastern sky was banded with silvery clouds as Zak followed Switch and the others away from the villa. They were carrying all their gear with them, including the micro-tents and camping equipment they had brought along for just this kind of emergency.

They headed south-east into the forested hills, keeping away from obvious tracks, forging a hard path through the dense trees. Every now and then Switch would stop, dropping to a crouch and giving them the signal to keep absolutely silent.

Zak stared anxiously through the trees as they moved deeper into the forest. This would be the perfect moment for Slingshot to make contact, he thought.

Jason? Where are you? We could really use some help right now.

Zak could hear the distant or not-so-distant sound of goat-bells. Sometimes he saw goats walking through the trees a little way off. Always in a narrow line, one following the other, their bells jangling in the early quiet of the day.

Zak knew that Switch was leading them in the general direction of Kharkhinos Cove – but there was a whole landscape of rugged hills and valleys between them and Rhea's lair.

It was almost zero-seven-hundred when Zak and the others came up a steep slope and found themselves in a small clearing among rearing shoulders of brown rock capped by wind-blown and twisted trees.

They made camp, setting up the tents and preparing themselves a quick breakfast.

Switch put Zak on watch. He moved as silently as possible around the perimeter of the small camp, watching intently, listening for any strange sounds. What was going to happen next? Just how smart was Reaperman? Were his people already on their tail?

Could the five of them really bring down his whole organization? What if Reaperman knew exactly where they were and decided to use SWORD on them?

Zak shuddered. Too creepy! Way too horrible to think about.

Moon appeared through the trees. Breakfast was ready and Switch wanted everyone together for a few minutes.

"Knowing exactly when Reaperman intends to hit London doesn't change our mission brief," Switch told them as they sat together eating and drinking in the morning light. "We can count on the fact that Slingshot will be given the new info. He knows how to contact us, so we need to be ready to move on his orders at a moment's notice. Meanwhile, we continue as planned."

"If we had scuba gear, we could launch an attack on that underwater hatch Silver and Moon found," said Jackhammer. "I'm itching to get my hands on those people down there."

"You're not the only one," said Switchblade. "But I'm not going to agree to some kind of suicidal assault on Base Hades just because we're feeling bad about Reaperman's goons taking us by surprise." He looked slowly from one to the next. "We have to be smarter than that. More professional. We were intending to try and find a way into Base Hades from the landward side today – and we're still going to do that. " He looked at the GPS app on his Mob. "Whether the waiter last night was Slingshot or not doesn't matter right now," he continued. "He gave us some good solid info about the best way of getting up into the hills above Kharkhinos Cove. We're going to use it."

"Do we stick together or split up?" asked Cat.

"For the time being, we keep together," Switch replied. His eyes flashed with determination as he looked at them. "We were caught out back at the villa," he said. "I don't intend that to happen again. Code Platinum alert at all times, guys. We have to get this right."

Zak was worn out and aching in every muscle by the time they had fought their way across the hills. By the looks of the others, they weren't doing any better. Even Hammer was struggling and he was strong, like the Hulk.

Zak wiped sweat out of his eyes. This was gruelling terrain, even for fit and well-trained agents. It was late morning now, and they had followed Oliver's hill-trekking advice all the way, keeping off the open tourist trails and using GPS to pinpoint their location.

At last, Switch called a halt and they waited in a weary

huddle while he went to scope out the way ahead. The GPS showed they were close to Reaperman's inlet. It was time to start watching out for more obvious danger signs.

Switch came gliding back through the trees. He crouched among them. "The fence Oliver told us about runs across our path about a hundred and fifty metres beyond the rise over there," he said. "It's just an ordinary wire-link fence from what I could see, but we'll have to deal with it if we're going to get any closer to Reaperman's hangout."

"Do you think it's electrified?" asked Moon.

"I saw a junction box of some kind attached to one of the posts, so we have to assume either it's electrified or it's wired to send an alarm signal if anyone tampers with it or tries to climb over it," said Switch. "We also have to work on the basis that Reaperman is expecting us."

"Let's not disappoint him," said Hammer, punching a fist into his palm. "I need some payback on the guy who gave me this headache."

"We're not geared up for a fight," said Switch. "We're here to gather intel and get it back to Fortress so they can pass it on to Slingshot."

"Why hasn't he made contact with us yet?" asked Zak. "I don't get it."

"Neither do I," said Switch.

"Maybe he prefers to work solo?" suggested Wildcat.

"Maybe something's happened to him," Hammer muttered darkly.

"Maybe we should stop wasting our time wondering about it and get on with the job?" said Moon.

"Agreed," said Switch. "No more questions. Let's do what we were sent here to do. Speed is going to work better than strength now." He turned to Zak. "Are you ready for this?" he asked.

"You bet," said Zak.

"Hammer and Moon and I will set up a diversion by the fence over there," Switch explained, pointing northwards. "Our job is to draw the attention of the guards away while you and Cat head south and get into Reaperman's compound any way you can. Make for the villa. We need photos of any buildings or bunkers or hatches – or anything that looks as if it might lead into Base Hades. If there's nothing, you're going to have to try and get into the villa itself. Use your Mobs – programme them so that any pictures you take will be sent straight to Fortress."

"And what if we find a way to get into Base Hades?" asked Cat.

Switch paused for a moment. "Go for it," he said.

"Are you sure?" asked Moon. "They could get caught."

"I know," Switch said. He glanced at his Mob. "It's thirteen-zero-seven now. Reaperman said the Awakening of Perses was set for zero-six-hundred tomorrow. That gives us less than fifteen hours."

Zak understood the danger Switch was sending them into. They had to infiltrate an enemy stronghold with no idea of how many people inhabited the place, or how acute their security systems were. The image of the Russian agent being killed by SWORD came into Zak's mind. Dr Zoli's voice came with it.

He was caught snooping on us.

He shuddered, seeing his own fears reflected in Hammer and Wildcat's eyes. He pushed his anxieties away. This was no time to panic. This was the time to call on all their training and expertise. This was the time to get the job done.

Zak stood up, slinging his backpack determinedly over his shoulder. He looked at Wildcat. "Ready?"

Zak and Cat peered out from the cover of the trees. Ahead of them lay an area of around twenty metres of open land, crossed by a two-metre-high wire fence.

They had a plan.

"Ready when you are," Zak said to Wildcat. He looked at her. "Nervous?" he asked.

"About getting over the fence without touching it?" She shook her head. "We can do it. No problem."

"No," Zak said. "I was thinking about the other thing."

"Oh. About the prospect of having my brain turned to rice pudding inside my head?" she replied. "No. Not at all." She looked into his eyes and he could read in her expression the same private terror that he was fighting to control. "Why do you ask?"

Zak shrugged, breaking her gaze. "Just wondered." He stood up, activating the heat-seeker app on his Mob. He pointed it at the fence, scanning the length of it. Nothing showed up. Good. That meant they had a window of opportunity to get over without being seen.

Zak turned to Cat and her image appeared on the Mob's screen as a vivid blaze of bright red. But there was something else. Unsure of exactly what he had seen, Zak stepped past Cat and scanned the trees.

A red flash showed among the blues and greens.

Not Switch or any of the others – they were off to Zak's right. Not an animal either – the red glow was upright. Human. Moving stealthily closer.

"We're being tailed," Zak hissed, dropping to a crouch.

"How many?" Cat murmured.

"I only saw one."

Cat tapped the Imp in her ear to activate it. "Switch?" she whispered. "We have incoming – behind us. Solo, we think."

She frowned, tapping the tiny transmitter again.

"We must be out of range," she said, looking at Zak. "We're on our own."

"Silver? Cat?" Switch frowned, touching a fingertip against his Imp. "Speak to me, guys. What's going on?" He looked uneasily at Hammer and Moon. "I'm getting nothing," he said. "Try your Mob, Moon."

Moon tapped a quick message and pressed Send. The message bounced back.

Failed.

"There must be something up here jamming the signals," said Moon. "Reaperman's no slouch when it comes to the high-tech equipment."

"That's what worries me," muttered Switch. "For all we know, we might already be in his cross-wires." He raised his head over the ridge and stared at the fence.

"I've got three ... four strong signals on the other side," said Hammer, aiming his Mob with the heat-seeker app activated.

"I can see them," said Switch. Three men were walking casually along about ten metres beyond the fence. There was no sign of weapons, although Switch was sure they'd have guns hidden away under their jackets.

The fourth man was further away, standing on a hump of land, facing Switch and the others, scanning the trees with binoculars.

"Silver and Cat should be in position by now," Switch said. "Go for it, Hammer."

Jackhammer was crouching over a pile of woodchips and leaves and ferns that they had gathered. He pushed the firelighter into it and triggered the flame. The heap smouldered for a few moments, then caught. Hammer sprinkled some water from a bottle over the pile.

The three agents backed away as the damp kindling sent plumes of smoke spiralling into the air. The man with the binoculars called to the others. They moved quickly towards the fence, and Switch saw one of them take a handgun from inside his jacket.

"Keep down," Switch muttered. "Let's see what happens next."

So far, the diversion seemed to be working. Now it was up to Silver and Cat.

*

Zak and Cat raced for the fence. They crossed the open ground at a sprint. Cat stood with her back to the fence, bracing her legs, linking her fingers to form a stirrup. Zak sprang, boosted by her hands. He sailed easily over the fence and came down lightly on the other side.

Now for the tricky part. He got up, watching Cat as she paced away from the fence. She was an outstanding athlete, he knew that. Pretty much Olympic level on a good day. She used the Fosbury flop method – which meant going over the fence backwards and head-first. It was Zak's job to catch her on the other side. If he got it wrong she could break her neck.

She paused, breathing slowly, focusing on the top of the fence. She rocked backwards and forwards on the balls of her feet. Then she went for it. Zak's heart was beating fast as he watched her take the run-up. She launched herself, curving her back. She flipped and suddenly she was coming down towards him.

Her shoulders smacked into his hands and he went crashing to the ground with Wildcat on top of him. They both lay gasping for a few moments. Most of Cat's weight had driven into Zak's stomach, and he could hardly breathe.

Cat rolled off and sprang to her feet. She held out a hand to Zak. They looked at each other. Then she gave a slight smile and nodded.

Job well done.

They ran away from the fence, keeping low, following the slope of the hill, heading into more trees. The land was dropping steeply now, falling away towards the northern headland of Kharkhinos Cove. Through the trees Zak caught occasional glimpses of the sea, far below.

They came to a knuckled fist of white rock. Keeping flat, they crawled to the edge and stared down.

"There it is," said Cat. Part-way down the long forested slope, Zak could see the tiled roofs of Achilles Rhea's villa. "You up for this?"

Zak nodded. "But if our signal is being blocked we won't be able to send any pictures back to Fortress," he pointed out. "That means we have to get out of here in one piece. This whole thing will be a waste of time if we're captured or . . ."

"*One* of us has to get out of there," Cat cut across him. "If we encounter any nasties, I'll engage them while you run for it."

"No way," said Zak.

She gave him a hard look. "You can run twice as fast as me," she said. "If things get tricky, I need to know you'll get any intel back to Fortress." She lifted an eyebrow.

"Do you think I can't look after myself, Silver?"

"I know you can," said Zak. "But . . ."

"Then let's get on with it." Without giving him time to argue, she slithered back along the rock and plunged into the trees.

"I am so *not* leaving you behind to get your brain mushed," Zak muttered under his breath as he ran to catch up with her. He aimed his Mob, scanning for heat signatures. There was no one close by. So far, so good. But now the hillside was getting even steeper and they had to be careful with their footing.

Suddenly Wildcat caught hold of Zak's shoulder. She pulled him behind a tree, her fingers to her lips. Gesturing back the way they had come, her mouth to his ear, she whispered, "There's someone there."

"It can't be the same person as before," hissed Zak. "He wouldn't have been able to get past the fence – not on his own."

"Whoever it is, we can't let ourselves be tracked," whispered Wildcat. "We have to take him out."

Zak slipped his backpack off his shoulders and pulled out a Taz. "I'll stay here," he said. "You go on. When he comes past I'll zap him. He won't know what hit him."

Cat nodded. She flicked a quick look around the tree trunk then got up and began to clamber down the hill.

Within a few seconds, she had vanished among the trees.

Zak stood with his back to the trunk, hardly breathing, listening intently.

He heard the crack of a twig. The rustle of low branches. He tasted blood in his mouth and realized he was biting his lip. Sounds of movement came closer.

He swallowed hard.

A man in green camouflage was coming past the tree, his face hidden behind a ski mask. Zak sprang forwards, aiming the Taz at the exposed skin at the side of the man's neck.

The man spun round, his arm scything back, knocking Zak's blow aside. The Taz went spinning into the undergrowth. Zak aimed a power-kick at the man's knee, hoping to take him down quickly, but the man jumped aside and the blow went wild. While Zak was trying to regain his balance, the heel of the man's hand drove into his sternum, knocking the breath out of his lungs.

Even as he stumbled, gasping, Zak brought his backpack round in a wide swing that struck the man on the side of the head. The man lost his footing, but he grabbed at Zak as he fell and the two of them went rolling down the hill in a flurry of dirt and twigs and undergrowth.

They crashed against a tree and lay tangled together, panting for breath. Zak was the first to stagger to his feet. A hand snatched at his ankle and he was tipped onto his face. He squirmed onto his back as the man came down on top of him, pinning his shoulders to the ground.

"Zachary, stop!" the man gasped. "It's me."

CHAPTER **EIGHT**

Zak stared up into the man's dark eyes. Beyond startled. Stunned. Disbelieving.

It was impossible.

"Dodge?" he murmured. "But . . ."

Another figure loomed over them. There was a brief crackle of electricity. Dodge slumped sideways with a groan. Wildcat stood there, a Taz in her fist.

"Gotcha!" she said.

"No, Cat!" cried Zak, scrambling to his feet. "He's not one of them. He's a friend." He leaned over the unconscious man, easing the ski mask up off his head, still hardly able to believe his eyes. "It's Dodge – my pal from London."

"You're kidding me?" said Wildcat. "The homeless guy? You can't be serious. No way."

"I'm telling you, it's him," insisted Zak.

He looked down at his friend. The heavy beard was gone and the hair had been cut short, but he would have known that face anywhere, with its hollow cheeks and deep-set eyes and high forehead.

"What would your tramp pal be doing on Panos?" Wildcat demanded. "And why would he be wearing official issue British Army woodland pattern DPMs?"

DPM was the commonly used term for camouflage uniform.

"I don't know," Zak said, searching in his backpack for a water bottle. "But he used to be in the army, I know that. Perhaps . . ." His voice faded. He couldn't think of any reason why Dodge should be here. Cat was right to be distrustful. It made no sense at all.

"Lift his head, I'm going to try and get him to drink," Zak said.

"We should tie him up first," said Cat.

"He's my friend," Zak said. "Surely we don't need to tie him up?"

"Have it your own way," said Cat. "But if he . . ."

Dodge's eyes flickered open. He groaned and put his hand to his neck. There was a small red burn where Wildcat's Taz had zapped him.

"Dodge, are you okay?" Zak asked.

"I'll be fine," Dodge groaned. "It's not the first time I've been tasered." He sat up. Cat stepped back, eyeing him warily.

"What are you doing here?" Zak asked urgently.

"Colonel Hunter sent me," said Dodge.

"I don't think so," said Cat. "He would have alerted us."

"I told him not to," said Dodge. "I asked him to let me make contact with Slingshot first." He frowned. "I arranged to meet Slingshot late last night, but he didn't show. I'm not sure what that means."

"You've been in contact with Slingshot?" Zak asked.

"Only briefly," said Dodge. "We exchanged call signs and co-ordinates for the meet. That's all. What about you?"

"Nothing so far," said Cat. She looked at Zak. "I'm not convinced about any of this," she said.

"Text Fortress the words 'Greek Philosopher'," said Dodge. "They'll text you back 'Diogenes'. That should prove that I'm here under your boss's orders."

"We can't," said Cat. "There's something blocking our signals."

"Then you'll just have to trust me for the time being," said Dodge.

Cat looked uneasily at Dodge.

Was Dodge telling them the whole the truth? Zak wondered. He looked into his friend's eyes. His doubts faded. Dodge was one of the good guys. He had to be here with Control's blessing.

"Trust me not at all, or all in all," Dodge said quietly.

Zak smiled, recognizing one of Dodge's quotes. "Who said that?" he asked.

"A great poet," Dodge began.

"It's Alfred, Lord Tennyson," interrupted Wildcat. Zak never stopped being surprised by the weird stuff Cat knew. She frowned then shook her head. "Okay, if Silver trusts you, I guess I have to give you the benefit of the doubt – for now. So, where do we go from here?"

"I'm guessing you're here to try and find a way into Base Hades," said Dodge.

"That's the plan," said Wildcat. "Are you here to help, or what? And, excuse me, why would Control send . . . I'm sorry . . . but I can't think of a better way of putting it. Why would Control send us a down-and-out?"

"Because this particular down-and-out used to be in the SAS," said Dodge. "And I have some experience and expertise that is going to help you with your mission."

He tried to get up, but his legs were still shaky from the taser shock. Zak helped him, his shoulder under Dodge's arm to support him. Dodge poured water from Zak's bottle over his head, then he swung his arms and stamped his feet a few times.

"I'd forgotten how unpleasant it was getting tasered," he said. He shook himself and stretched his arms. "Okay, I have some new information. We need to get out of here. This isn't the way to get into Base Hades. I've found a better one. Where are the others?"

"Back up the hill," said Zak. "They created a diversion so we could get over the fence without Reaperman's people seeing us."

"Speaking of which, how did *you* get over the fence?" asked Cat.

"Tricks of the trade," said Dodge. "I'll show you on the way back. Come on, we need to link up with the rest of the team. We have work to do."

"I don't take orders from you," said Cat. "Not until I have confirmation from Fortress about exactly who you are."

"Cat, we can trust him," said Zak.

"Fine," Cat said reluctantly. She glowered at Dodge. "But I'm keeping my Taz handy, and if I get suspicious, you're going down again, my friend. Got that?"

"Got it," said Dodge. "Come on. The clock's ticking."

They made their way to the fence. A small hole had been cut in the chain-links close to the ground. Insulated wires with tiny clamps on each end had been attached to the severed links.

Zak understood immediately what Dodge had done. The wires kept the electrical current flowing so that the alarm wouldn't be tripped when the fence was cut.

Smart move.

Very SAS!

They slithered under the fence then ran for the trees.

"We need to find the rest of the team," said Dodge. "I've found a place where we can debrief everyone and let Colonel Hunter know I've made contact with you. We've still got time to get this done if we move fast." He looked sharply at Cat. "Are you with me?"

She nodded. "I'll go and get Switch and the others," she said. "You stay here."

She disappeared into the trees.

Dodge sat with his back to a trunk. He looked at Zak, standing in front of him. "Well, Zachary," he said. "Who'd have guessed we'd end up on a mission together?"

That was quite a question. Zak didn't entirely know

how he felt about it yet. Dodge looked so different – clean-shaven and wearing an army uniform – that it was difficult to think of him as the grubby old tramp who lived in the arches under Waterloo Station. But Dodge seemed entirely at home here, in his element. As though the soldier in him had never entirely gone away.

Zak grinned, masking his thoughts. "It's really good to see you," he said cautiously. "But did Colonel Hunter tell you how bad this might get? Did he tell you about Reaperman?"

"Your chief told me all that I need to know about Operation Icarus," Dodge replied. "Including how much it will mean to you and your brother when Reaperman is brought down." He smiled. "When danger approaches, sing to it," he added. "That's an old Arabic proverb, Zachary. It means if you face danger without fear, you're more likely to survive."

"I like the sound of that," said Zak. "Dodge? Why didn't Jason . . . I mean, Slingshot . . . why didn't he meet you?"

Dodge looked at him thoughtfully. "I don't know," he said. "I can think of several reasons, and none of them need to be bad news. I was out of contact with my base for three straight days once. I had to go dark because the enemy was getting too close. Maybe Slingshot's lying low for the same reason. You shouldn't worry about it, Zak. Your brother's survived in the field for nearly three years. He knows what he's doing."

Zak looked at his friend. "Why did you stop being a soldier?" He hesitated. "And how did the Colonel convince you to . . ." he made a gesture, indicating the camouflaged uniform, ". . . you know. Start it up again?"

"He had one very convincing argument," said Dodge. "He told me you needed me." He rubbed his chin. "And as for your other question, that's a long story, and not one I'm going to tell you now."

"But you will tell me, at some point?" asked Zak.

"I will," said Dodge. "That's a promise."

Dodge led them in a south-westerly direction through the hills. At first, Switch and the others had been as uneasy about Dodge's sudden appearance on Panos as Wildcat had been, but once they were out of range of the jamming devices Reaperman had set up over Kharkhinos Cove, Switch was able to text the words "Greek Philosopher" to Fortress. The reply came back almost immediately.

Diogenes.

Proof that Dodge was here under Colonel Hunter's orders.

"What do we call you?" asked Switch as Dodge pushed on at a rapid pace through the dense trees. "What's your real name?"

"Dodge will do," came the reply. "That's real enough."

Zak noticed the others exchanging puzzled glances. It didn't surprise him that they weren't certain about taking their lead from Dodge. None of them had met him before and it must be weird following a man who had been living rough under the arches at Waterloo Station for the past few years. Almost as weird as it was for Zak himself!

But Dodge had already proven himself capable of swift and decisive action. He'd helped Zak when London had been under threat of the Burning Sky device. He'd taken out two dangerous men without a moment's hesitation. Dodge was good in a crisis – Zak knew it was only a matter of time before the others realized that.

It was late afternoon when they stepped out of the trees and found themselves looking at an old, abandoned stone building. A black MPV was parked alongside the dilapidated house and Zak saw a narrow track winding away through the forest.

"It's best to keep out of the house," Dodge advised

them. "It looks as though the roof could come down at any moment. Everything we need is in the van."

He clicked a small remote and the side door of the vehicle slid open.

Most of the passenger seats had been removed, and the rear of the MPV was filled with boxes and bags.

"Make yourselves comfortable," said Dodge, climbing in.

"What *is* all this gear?" asked Hammer, sitting on one of the boxes.

"What you're sitting on is explosives," Dodge replied. "The rest is some kit we'll be needing."

Hammer gave him a startled look and moved off the box.

"How did you get it here?" asked Moon.

"On an Islander BN2T Mark 2 out of RAF Northolt," Dodge said, reaching under the driver's seat and pulling out a slim black bag. "We landed at Panos International yesterday evening. I commandeered the van and used GPS to bring it here."

"And why here in particular?" asked Switch.

Dodge sat on the floor of the van and drew a laptop out of the black bag. "Because this is the closest I could get to the cave system," he said, opening the laptop and tapping the keyboard to bring it to life.

"What cave system?" asked Wildcat. "No one told us about . . ."

Dodge raised his hand to silence her. "This can't be good," he said. "There are twelve Flashes from Fortress."

Flash signals were not routine. Colonel Hunter only sent the emergency Flash signal if something urgent or serious had happened.

Dodge twisted the laptop round so that they could all see the screen.

The familiar square P17 logo appeared for a moment, then they found themselves looking at Colonel Hunter's grim face.

"Sergeant Carter, I've been trying to contact you for the past two hours," barked the Colonel.

Wow! Dodge's real last name was Carter, thought Zak. And he was a sergeant.

"Sorry, sir, I've been busy making contact with your agents," Dodge replied. "I didn't think it was prudent to take the laptop with me, in case of problems."

"Have you linked up with Slingshot?" demanded the Colonel.

"No, sir. We arranged a meet, but he didn't show."

"Slingshot has missed his last two contact times," said the Colonel. "We have to assume there's a problem. Slingshot is MIA, Sergeant Carter. You can no longer rely on help from him. Do you understand me?"

"Yes, sir," said Dodge.

Zak went cold. MIA – that meant *Missing In Action*. It meant captured or . . .

The vivid image of the dead Russian agent came into his head. Might Jason have already met the same horrible fate?

"Do you think he's been killed?" Zak blurted.

"I have no information on that subject, Agent Quicksilver," said the Colonel. "Switchblade, you will consider yourself under Sergeant Carter's command from now on. All of you. Be smart and be safe. Fortress out." Just before the screen went blank, Zak saw a look of anxious compassion flicker across Colonel Hunter's face.

He thinks Jason is dead.

No! No way. I'd know.

Would you?

Really?

Zak struggled against the conflicting voices in his head. He looked at his companions. Their faces were pale and . . . haunted. As if they'd already made their minds up about what had happened to Jason.

"He's not dead," Zak said, hoping that saying the words out loud would convince him he was right.

Dodge rested his hand on Zak's trembling shoulder. "Whatever's happened, we have to work on the basis that Slingshot is out of the loop for the time being," he said. "We have work to do. Moonbeam? There's a pouch down beside you – it has a map in it. Take it out, please. There's something you all need to see."

Moon spread the map out on the floor of the van. It was a highly detailed map of the northern half of Panos, and someone had drawn lines and circles on it in red magic marker.

"We're here," said Dodge, stabbing a finger close to the group of red circles. "The rings indicate a cluster of caves. I've spoken to a local caver and I used the information he gave me to mark the cave systems that run under the island." They all leaned in closer. "Colonel Hunter's original plan was that we should approach Base Hades from the sea. My speciality in the SAS was underwater work. You people were meant to create a diversion so I could enter Kharkhinos Cove using a CCUBA and blow the hatch you found. Then my job was to find SWORD and destroy it, while you were keeping Reaperman and his cronies busy. I have a limpet mine as well as ordinary PE4 to get the job done."

Limpet mines were magnetic explosive devices that could be attached to the hulls of ships below the waterline then detonated to sink them. PE4 was a plastic explosive – very useful in the field. A small amount could get you through a plate-steel door, and the good thing about PE4 was that it couldn't go off accidentally. It needed a detonator.

"I'm sorry," said Zak. "I don't know what CCUBA means."

"It stands for Closed Circuit Underwater Breathing Apparatus," said Wildcat. "It's like a scuba diving set, but it doesn't leave a trail of bubbles."

Dodge stabbed his finger at the map again. "These caves lead to an underground river that will take me all the way to Kharkhinos Cove," he said. "That way, I can get to Base Hades without a boat. Reaperman will be expecting us to come at him either by land or by sea – but he won't be looking for anyone popping up right under his nose."

"Are you sure he doesn't know about these caves?" asked Jackhammer. "He could have a security system installed down there."

"If he has, I'll deal with it," said Dodge. "But I'm not going in alone. I'll need back-up. Switchblade and Quicksilver will be coming with me."

Zak felt a shiver of apprehension. He would never say anything, but he didn't like caves. The thought of being stuck under the ground in a small stone hole frightened the life out of him.

"Moonbeam, I want you to lead the others up into the hills again," Dodge continued. "I'll give you some PE4 and some thunder-flashes and smoke bombs. Make some noise, okay? Let Reaperman think we're coming from above. It needs to look real."

"We can do that," said Moon. "When do we start?"

"Hold off until we get to the cove," said Dodge. "Then let it rip."

"Problem," said Hammer, lifting his hand. "They're jamming our signals – how will we know when you're in position?"

Dodge narrowed his eyes. "Good point," he said. He leaned over the map again, his finger following the red magic marker line, his lips moving soundlessly as though he was making calculations under his breath. "I want you to start the diversion at zero-four-hundred tomorrow. We'll be in position by then," he said at last. "We should all sleep for a few hours now, if we can. We head off at midnight."

Zak managed to snatch a total of about ten minutes' sleep before he heard Dodge moving about the cramped and crowded van. He looked at his Mob. It was 23:45. He could see Wildcat's face dimly lit by the screen of her own Mob. He guessed she was playing one of her complicated logic games. He obviously hadn't been the only one having trouble getting to sleep. Switch and Moon were also wide-eyed in the gloom. Only Jackhammer was fast asleep; he had to be shaken to wake him up.

There wasn't much conversation as they got ready to set off on their missions. The packets of PE4 were divided up and Moon's team were given the thunder-flashes and smoke bombs they'd need to make it look as though the attack was coming from the hills.

Switch, Zak and Dodge had heavier loads to carry. They each had a backpack crammed with equipment, as well as a holdall containing the heavy and cumbersome CCUBA kits.

They climbed out of the van. The night was cloudy and cool. Wind rippled through the trees. Zak felt strangely apprehensive. The thought of the caves and the underground river was worrying, of course, but what really gnawed at his mind was the constant fear that something terrible had happened to his brother. It was agonizing to think that Jason might have been captured – or even killed by that horrible reptile Dr Zoli. Zak couldn't bear the thought of his brother being murdered when they were so close to finally meeting one another.

And Jason was just one person – how many millions more might die if SWORD was unleashed on the unsuspecting people of London? It made his heart ache when he thought about how much depended on their mission being successful. He just hoped that his unease didn't show in his face. He was determined not to let Dodge and the others down.

"See you later, then," said Moon, hefting her backpack onto her shoulders. "Break a leg, okay?"

"You too," said Switch.

Zak's mouth was dry and there was a scratchiness in his throat.

"The game's afoot," Dodge said quietly. "Follow your spirit, and upon this charge cry 'God for Harry, England, and Saint George'."

Wildcat smiled grimly. "Shakespeare," she said. "*Henry the Fifth*, act three, scene one."

Dodge nodded.

Was there anything that girl didn't know?

Dodge turned and walked away. Switch and Zak followed him in silence. Zak glanced back and saw Moon and the others disappearing into the trees. He wondered if he would ever see them again.

Of course you will. Stop thinking like that. Idiot.

It was hard work, carrying their equipment through the trees in the darkness. Roots snagged their feet and branches slapped them in the face, and all Zak could hear over the rustle of their movements was the sound of his blood pulsing in his temples.

Dodge led them to a rocky outcrop among the trees. Fists of grey stone stood up around them.

"This is it," said Dodge, putting his holdall down. He pointed to a dark slot among the rocks. "According to what I've been told, the cave slopes down for several metres before there's a drop of about twenty-five metres to the next level." He crouched, pulling his backpack off and taking out some tough nylon rope. "The tunnels become level then, but there are some awkward narrow stretches, so we'll have to be careful not to damage the equipment as we go through." He drew out a hard hat with a lamp attached to the front. "I've tested the batteries and we should have enough light to get us there without any problems," he said. "Once we get past the narrows, we'll hit a large flooded cavern. That's where things will start to get tricky."

Zak eyed the cave mouth. He had the feeling things would get tricky for him a long time before they hit the water.

CHAPTER **NINE**

"Are you okay?" Dodge's voice had an odd, booming quality to it.

"Yes, fine," Zak called back. "No problem."

He was wedged in a tight gap between two pincers of stone. He felt around blindly below for the next foothold, his fingers going numb as he gripped the ledge above. Apart from the difficulty of moving at all in the vertical shaft, he was finding it hard to climb without being able to see where he was going. The stone shaft was too narrow for him to angle his own helmet-light down, and if Switch shone his light upwards, Zak was dazzled by it.

"The next foothold is down a bit and off to your right," Switch called from close below. "You're almost there."

Zak felt a hand grasp his ankle and move his foot to one side. His toes found the ledge. He tested his weight on it then let himself drop. His whole body seemed to be running with cold sweat. His fingers were slick with it, and so was his forehead. He had to keep pausing to wipe it out of his eyes.

"That's it," came Dodge's voice again. "You're past the worst bit. Don't worry; if you slip, the rope will take your weight."

The rope was anchored to the rock with a small metal crampon. Zak felt like a fly clinging to a wall. Muscles straining. Stomach churning. Fingers losing all feeling.

"The next foothold is to the left," said Switch.

Zak stretched his leg down. He couldn't wait for this part of the mission to be over.

"There you go," said Switch. "That wasn't so bad, was it?"

Zak gave him a relieved grin.

They had come to the foot of the shaft at long last. Zak glanced at his Mob and was surprised to see that the descent had only taken twenty minutes. He felt as though he'd endured at least a couple of days in that endless chimney of rock.

They were in a small circular chamber – a little bubble of air, deep under the ground. Zak refused to let himself think of the thousands upon thousands of tons of rock bearing down on them.

Dodge was crouching by the wall with his back to them. All their equipment was piled up in the middle of the sandy floor. Wiping his face with his sleeve, Zak looked around. Something was puzzling him.

In every direction the stone walls plunged straight down to the sandy floor. There didn't seem to be a way out.

"Dodge?" he asked. "Where do we go from here?"

Dodge stood up and stepped to one side. He pointed to a narrow dark slot at the foot of the wall.

Zak stared at the small gap. "Oh, you have got to be kidding me," he said.

"The passageway is only narrow like that for a couple of metres," Dodge said. "Then it widens out. We'll even be able to walk upright for part of the way. But we'll need to keep our wits about us – apparently it gets quite steep in places."

"How do we get the gear through?" asked Switch, and Zak was relieved to hear a catch in his voice. At least he wasn't the only one who had a problem with enclosed spaces.

"We'll attach the backpacks to one ankle by a strap," Dodge said, sounding amazingly calm and matter-of-fact about it. "We'll have to push the holdalls along ahead of us through the narrow parts." He gave them a reassuring smile. "I've been in tighter places than this," he said. "Just be sure to keep a good hold on the equipment bags. Don't let them fall – if the scuba gear gets damaged, we've wasted our time." He knelt, knotting a strap of his backpack around his ankle then taking hold of one of the bulky holdalls and pushing it into the slot. "I'll see you guys at the other end," he said.

Zak watched as Dodge eased himself into the hole. The backpack jerked and bounced as it disappeared.

Zak's mouth was uncomfortably dry.

"Switch?" he croaked. "I'm really not . . ."

Switch dropped to his knees, knotting his backpack to his ankle. "Tell me on the other side," he said. He looked up, giving Zak a quick wink. "Glad you joined Project 17?"

Zak opened his mouth but couldn't think of anything to say. He watched as Switch wriggled into the tunnel.

He was alone. He could hear shuffling and kicking and scraping noises from the tunnel mouth.

He knotted his backpack to his leg and shoved the holdall into the hole.

"I'm going to nail this," he muttered under his breath. "That's all I want to say." He lay flat, pushing the heavy holdall on ahead of him as he edged into the tunnel. "One way or another – I am definitely going to get through this."

"Have some water," said Dodge. "I think we've all earned a drink."

Zak took the bottle from Dodge and swallowed about half its contents in one long gulp. His clothes felt as if they'd been glued to his body by grit and dirt. He was filthy and sweaty and disgusting. He had dirt in his hair and down his back, in his shoes and up his sleeves. The fine grit seemed to have got everywhere, chafing and rubbing his skin and making every movement unpleasant.

An hour had passed since Zak had squeezed through that impossible tunnel mouth. An hour of discomfort and fear and pain and grindingly hard work. But despite everything, they had got through and now Zak had a few moments to feel relieved and giddy and light-headed.

"I've got sand everywhere," said Switch, plucking at

his clothes. "I've got sand in places I didn't even know I had places."

They were in a huge, spectacular cavern, sitting together on a ledge above a wide lake of still, clear water.

As they looked around, the light from their helmets gleamed and flashed on great pendulous stalactites that hung from the roof, glowing with a translucent creamy radiance. Thick, glittering stalagmites rose out of the water, each with its own perfect inverted reflection. The whole cavern looked as though it had been made of molten candle wax.

Under any other circumstances, Zak would have found this place amazing and wonderful. Right now, all he could think about was the fact that their only way out of here was going to be through the lake.

After a brief rest, Dodge began to unload the holdalls.

"Normally, I'd insist on a full wetsuit for this kind of diving," Dodge told them. "But that's not an option. I've brought along some waterproof bags for your shoes and anything else that shouldn't get wet, but you'll have to keep your jeans and T-shirts on. I'm warning you now – the water is going to be cold. Very cold."

They spent a few minutes becoming familiar with the breathing apparatus, then it was time to get ready for the dive. They helped one another into the CCUBA gear. Each of them had a torch strapped to their wrist.

Dodge was carrying a bag with the limpet mine in it. Switch had a bag containing the PE4, carefully wrapped in a waterproof container. Zak's bag held all the other things they'd need.

Dodge sat on the lip of the ledge, tightening the straps on his flippers. He looked round at them, the facemask on his head.

"Keep in line and stay close," he told them. "I'll go first. Silver next, then Switch. We're going to be underwater for some time, so keep calm and always breathe slow and steady. The water here is still, but you should expect some currents and undertows as we go along. If I think it's getting bad, I'll rope us together, but I don't want to do that unless I have to, in case the rope gets snagged." He pulled the mask over his face, fitted the mouthpiece and slid down into the water. Zak pulled his own facemask into position. Switch looked a little bit blurry through the glass. He gave Zak the okay sign – thumb and first finger curled into an O. Zak pushed the breathing tube into his mouth. It was strange and uncomfortable at first, but he'd been given scuba-diving lessons a few months ago – it was a normal part of Project 17 training – so he knew more or less what to expect.

He shuffled to the rim of the ledge and eased himself into the water.

The cold took Zak's breath away for a few moments. He saw Dodge bobbing in the water a little way off. He heard a soft splash and turned to see Switch in the water behind him.

Dodge swam across the lake, avoiding the stalagmites, sending out ripples that broke the perfect reflection of the cave's high roof. Then he dived. Zak followed, trying to ignore the biting chill of the water.

Dodge was heading for a dark hole under the waterline. With a sudden flurry of flippers, he jetted forwards. Zak turned his head, giving Switch the A-Okay sign again. Switch nodded and responded with his own sign.

Breathing steadily, Zak followed Dodge into the underwater passage.

Zak had never experienced anything so eerie and disturbing in his life. All he could hear was the amplified sound of his own breathing. All he could see in the wavering light of his wrist-torch were the walls of the tunnel gliding by and the steady up-and-down rhythm of Dodge's flippers about two metres ahead of him.

Every now and then he would twist his head to look back and make sure Switch was still close behind. Yes, he was right there, swimming along determinedly.

They exchanged the A-Okay sign again.

Zak took long, deep breaths. He'd pushed away his fear now and he knew he'd make it.

Very slowly, centimetre by centimetre, the walls and the roof of the flooded tunnel opened out. Zak began to swim more strongly. It was almost over. Suddenly the roof soared away and Dodge turned round so he was facing Zak. He gestured upwards with his thumb.

Switch came to swim alongside them and they began to swim up a wide chimney of stone. Their torches flashed over ridges of white rock.

Zak couldn't be sure if he was just getting used to it, but the water didn't seem quite so cold any more. And now he could see patches of green – algae and seaweed. And small fish, darting into cover as they passed.

The shaft levelled out and Dodge swam towards a dark fissure in the wall and vanished into the crack. Switch and Zak followed. Switch punched Zak's arm and gave a double A-Okay sign. Zak nodded and they swam through the gap.

✼

"That was awesome!" panted Switch. "I've never . . . I mean . . . wow! What a rush."

Zak was relieved and exhausted and absolutely wired by his experience in the underwater caves.

The three of them were huddled together in waist-deep water at the furthermost point of Kharkhinos Cove. Clouds streaked across the night sky. In the dark, Zak could make out the ghostly white shape of the *Cerberus* and the black bulk of the freighter. There were no lights on either vessel. Up on the black, tree-shrouded hillside, a few lights glimmered, revealing the location of Achilles Rhea's villa.

"We've done well so far," said Dodge. He checked the waterproof watch on his wrist. "Zero-three-forty-five," he said. "We have fifteen minutes before Moonbeam and the others start the diversion. Once I've blown the hatch, one of us needs to stay back and keep our escape route open while the other two head into the base." He looked from Zak to Switch. "Any volunteers?"

"It can't be Silver," said Switch. "We're going to need his speed. I know how to use PE4 – I think I should go with him. We've worked together before – we make a good team. I don't want to be disrespectful . . . Mr . . . uh . . . Dodge . . . you've done amazingly well so far, but you haven't been involved in anything like this for years. You're bound to be rusty."

Dodge gave a strange, crooked smile. "And I'm old and past it?" he said.

Switch flushed. "I didn't mean that."

Dodge lifted his hand. "No, you're right. The two of you are a team – you should stay together. I'll watch your backs." He looked at his watch again. "Okay. Time's up. Let's go." He pulled his facemask back on and put his breathing tube into his mouth. He gave them a last look then slipped under the water.

Zak fitted his facemask. He felt strangely calm. He'd already accomplished the impossible over the past few hours. He was beginning to believe they might survive this mission after all.

Moon and Cat and Hammer were lying low in the trees on the hill close to Achilles Rhea's fence. Cat was using the heat-seeker app on her Mob to scope the area for signs of life while Moon and Hammer checked and re-checked their small arsenal of weapons.

"I can see two . . . three guys on the far side of the fence," Cat said. She looked up. Clouds were moving fast across the sky. The wind whistled in the trees. It was almost zero-four-hundred-hours. "Do you think Switch and the others are in position yet?"

"That Dodge guy seems to know what he's doing," said Moon. "I'd say they're right on target." She handed Hammer a small pack of PE4. "Get busy," she said. "It's time."

Hammer belly-crawled across the open ground towards the fence. Cat kept close watch from cover with her heat-seeker. No, it didn't seem as if the guards had noticed him. That wasn't going to last long. Pretty soon they'd have plenty to notice.

When Hammer had finished he twisted round and crawled rapidly back. Still the three figures glowing red on the screen of Cat's Mob didn't make any moves that suggested they'd seen him.

"Fire in the hold!" said Hammer, getting to his feet and standing behind a tree.

Cat braced herself. There was a sudden flash of light and a loud explosion. Smoke billowed up. Earth and stones rained down.

"Go! Go! Go!" yelled Moon.

The three of them raced for the fence.

The diversion had begun.

✳

Zak and Switch were treading water while Dodge swam through the rusty steel girders towards the hatch. They had turned off their torches – they couldn't risk lights being spotted in the inlet.

Suddenly, Dodge was swimming back towards them. Fast. He put his hands flat against either side of his head, covering his ears. Zak and Switch did the same. A few moments later there was a loud *whumph!* A bloom of red light burst out, boiling the water, sending shockwaves that buffeted them about and made Zak's ears ring.

Dodge gestured to them and they moved forwards.

The mine had ripped the hatch open. Zak swam through the entrance with Switch hard on his heels. Switch turned on his wrist-torch. They were in a small flooded chamber with another round hatch in the ceiling. The hatch had a wheel on its underside, like the hatches Zak had seen on submarines.

Zak turned and saw Dodge's face. He pointed upwards and gave a thumbs-up.

Switch swam to the hatch and began to turn the wheel. The hatch came swinging down. Bright light shone on the surface of the water. Switch pushed upwards and disappeared. Zak looked back at Dodge once more. It was impossible to guess his expression. Zak turned away and swam towards the ring of bright light.

After being submerged for so long, he felt strangely heavy and clumsy as Switch pulled him through the hatch and out of the water. They were in another small circular chamber, but this time with a bulkhead door to one side. They helped one another out of their scuba-diving gear. Their clothes were saturated and they were both freezing cold, but there was nothing they could do about that. They would just have to deal with it.

Switch quickly checked the contents of his bag. "The PE4 looks fine," he said. Zak emptied his own bag. The Mobs had survived and so had the thunder-flashes and SGD706/E03s that they had brought along. The SGDs were known as whizzers. They were small black balls that turned into shrieking smoke bombs when primed. Zak had used one before, and he knew how effective they could be.

They pulled on their shoes.

Switch went to the door and listened.

"I don't hear anything," he said. "Are you ready for this?"

Zak nodded.

It was strange – all his earlier anxiety seemed to have faded away. He was on dry land with a solid floor under his feet. He felt in control again.

Switch brought the lever down and swung the metal

door open. They stepped into a corridor. The floor was steel mesh but the walls had been hacked roughly out of solid stone. Zak had seen something exactly like this before – on the video that the German agent Isabel had smuggled out.

He was reminded suddenly of the terrible effects of the SWORD device.

No. This is no time to think about that stuff. Just do your job.

They moved silently along the corridor. It sloped upwards, lit by halogen tubes along the rocky ceiling. There were metal steps leading to a door with a circular glass panel.

Switch peered though the panel. He shook his head, meaning he couldn't see anyone. There was no handle on this side of the door – just a keypad attached to the wall beside it.

Switch took out his Mob, activated its decoder app and pressed it against the pad. Numbers whirled on the screen. There was a small ping as the numbers stopped. 0794658. Switch pressed the code and the door slid into the wall with a soft hiss.

Very high-tech.

They stepped into another corridor. No guards. Raw stone walls. Doors led off on either side.

"Is it me or is this too easy?" murmured Switch.

"Maybe Moon's diversion is working better than we thought," suggested Zak hopefully.

The door snapped shut behind them. The lock clicked with an ominously sharp noise.

"This is all wrong," said Switch. "We have to get out of here." He spun round, reaching for the keypad on this side.

Too late.

In both directions along the corridor, doors burst open. Black-uniformed men poured out, some armed with automatic machine guns. They came slowly towards Zak and Switch.

Trapped.

CHAPTER **TEN**

"Hi, guys," said Switch, his voice perfectly calm as the men approached along the corridor. "We were looking for the toilets, but I think we took a wrong turn somewhere."

Zak stood at his side, trembling slightly – not with fear but with a sudden adrenaline rush. He knew the effects well – the slightly rusty taste in his mouth, the feeling that he was about to burst right out of his skin. A clarity in his mind that was like nothing else in the world. The sensation that everything around him had slowed down.

He saw everything in the corridor with pinpoint accuracy, and he knew in an instant what he was going to do. Reaperman's thugs had made one big mistake. They had come from both sides – which meant they'd have to be careful about firing their machine guns in case they shot each other.

"Switch! Take the ones on the right!" he yelled. A fraction of a second later, Zak leaped forwards, bouncing high off the far wall, his hand in his bag, grabbing at a whizzer as he hurtled towards the group of men that were coming from the left-hand side of the corridor.

He rebounded back and forth across the corridor, his brain working as fast as his body, knowing where he was going to land next three moves ahead of himself. He caught a glimpse of Switch flinging himself at the other bunch of men, feet and fists flying.

Zak's feet hammered into the chest of one of the leading men, sending him crashing backwards, knocking the others aside like skittles.

Using the momentum of his jump, he launched himself high, ducking his head to avoid hitting the roof of the corridor, bringing one foot down onto the shoulder of a man and using it as a stepping stone.

He was vaguely aware of shouting voices and snatching hands, but he was past them in a flash, landing in a tight, controlled roll. He twisted the whizzer to prime it, and before he had even come to a halt, sent it skidding across the floor towards their attackers.

He flung his hands over his ears. There was a loud, high-pitched shriek and a plume of white smoke filled the corridor. Ear-splitting bangs and whistles erupted as the whizzer did its thing.

He sprang to his feet, feeling in his bag for a thunder-flash, his brain whirring, his body pumped. A man came staggering out of the smoke. Zak landed a Krav Maga kick to the man's knee, bringing him down, then leaping over him.

Bring it on!

Another man emerged from the smoke, aiming his gun. Zak whirled, knocking the gun out of his hands with a high roundhouse kick. A third man lunged forwards. Zak ducked, then pushed upwards, his shoulder smacking into the man's abdomen, lifting him off his feet and sending him thumping to the ground. But the move ripped Zak's backpack off and sent it skidding out of reach.

A hand grabbed at Zak's arm but he somersaulted, twisting free, bounding away again, fizzing with energy.

It was as if all the rage and the frustration that had been building up in him ever since he'd been told about Reaperman were exploding in one unstoppable eruption of furious action.

The noise of the whizzer stopped suddenly – Zak assumed someone must have smashed it. And the smoke was clearing faster than he'd expected. Of course! This base was underground – it must have a high-end air conditioning system that was sucking the smoke out.

A shout sounded from further along the corridor.

"Stop now or we kill him!"

Zak hesitated.

Switch?

A man stepped forwards through the swirling smoke. He had Switch in a vicious neck-hold. A knife was pressed to the side of his neck. There was blood on Switch's lip and one of his eyes was half-closed and swollen.

Switch looked up at Zak. There was anguish and self-disgust on his face. As if he thought he'd let Zak down.

Zak raised his hands.

Two men bore down on him from behind, forcing him onto his front, wrenching his arms behind his back. A knee drove into his spine, making him gasp in pain.

Another man approached, his boot only a millimetre from Zak's face. Zak braced himself for a kick in the mouth.

"Get him to his feet," snapped the man.

Zak was hauled up, his arms still locked behind his back. He stared into the man's face, too angry to be afraid.

The man raised his gun high, the butt end looming over Zak's head.

"Don't harm him," said a voice that Zak had heard before. A deep, gravelly voice, with a strong Greek accent.

Reaperman.

Zak twisted his head as Achilles Rhea walked slowly along the corridor from behind him. He was dressed in a smart grey suit and seemed unperturbed by what had just happened.

"So, then," he said, glancing at Switch then turning to look Zak up and down. "What have we here? Children playing at spies?" he smiled. "I'm guessing you must be some of Hunter's little boys." He paused in front of Zak. "Don't reproach yourselves for failing," he said smoothly. "You did very well to get this far." He smiled. "Your friends up in the hills did not fare so well, I'm afraid. They're all dead."

A cold horror filled Zak. Moon? Hammer? Wildcat? Dead?

Switch struggled, swearing loudly.

The knife bit deeper against his neck and he became still again, glaring at Rhea with undisguised loathing.

"You are young, even for one of Hunter's brats," said Rhea. He reached out and lifted Zak's chin with his fingers. "What are you? Twelve?"

"I'm fourteen," Zak said, determined not to lose control.

"My apologies," said Rhea. "Such a baby face." He spoke to the man holding Zak. "Take them away. We can deal with them later."

"I just want to say one thing," said Zak.

Rhea looked at him, his eyebrows arched questioningly.

"You're going to be brought down," Zak said levelly. "And I'm going to be there when it happens."

"An admirable ambition," said Rhea. "But unlikely to be fulfilled." He paused, holding Zak's gaze. "Such hatred," he said. "Hunter trains his children well."

"The Colonel didn't have to teach me to hate you," spat Zak. "I hated you from the moment I learned that you killed my parents."

"Did you, indeed?" said Rhea. "How very zealous of you. And who were your parents?"

"Janet and John Trent," said Zak.

Rhea looked thoughtful for a few moments then shook his head. "The names mean nothing to me, boy."

Zak stared at him. "My mother was an MI5 agent – she

was getting too close so you made her plane crash," he said in a rush. "You killed her in cold blood. Fourteen years ago. In Canada."

"I have ordered the deaths of many people," Rhea said lightly. "I can't be expected to remember all of their names."

A wild anger surged through Zak. He strained against the man holding him. "You must!" he shouted. "You must remember!"

Rhea laughed. "Truly, I don't," he said. "But I'm sure they died well in the service of their country. I dare say you should be proud of them." He patted Zak's cheek then turned on his heel and strode away.

Zak stared after him. Thunderstruck.

Reaperman had murdered Zak's parents like anyone else might swat irritating flies and he didn't even remember.

"Lock them both up," Rhea called back. "Put them with the other one. We'll deal with them later. The deadline is approaching. Perses will awaken soon. This will be a glorious day, my friends. A glorious day."

Wildcat ran through the trees, leaping over roots and rocks, her arms out for balance as she plunged down the steep hillside. She could hear someone close by, also crashing through the trees. Hammer, she guessed by the racket. Moon moved a lot more quietly.

There was shouting from behind. The occasional gunshot echoed through the forest. If their diversion had been intended to draw Reaperman's guards, then it had worked. There must be at least twenty men chasing them.

Their initial charge through the fence had brought down the three men on the other side. Cat and Hammer had quickly tied and gagged them, while Moon flung thunder-flashes and whizzers in all directions to create as much noise and smoke and confusion as possible.

It had not been long before more men had arrived. That was when things had got tricky. Automatic weapon-fire raked the hills. Cat and the others had raced for the cover of the trees, bullets kicking up spits of earth at their heels.

Wildcat had used up her supply of weapons. Now she was just running to keep Reaperman's thugs busy – and to survive. A dark figure appeared ahead of her through the trees.

She came to a skidding halt and darted to one side. Then she heard a gunshot and an instant later felt a searing pain in her left arm. She staggered, gasping in agony, slapping her hand to her arm. There was blood.

Biting back a cry, she stumbled and fell headlong into the bracken as the gunman ran up the hill towards her.

Her head was swimming with the pain.

She just hoped they'd caused enough mayhem up here to give Switch and the others the opportunity they needed to get into Base Hades undetected.

At least that would make the sacrifice worthwhile.

Zak made the men holding him fight every step as he and Switch were dragged away. They came to a metal door. Zak could see that there was blood trickling down Switch's T-shirt from the knife that was still being held against his throat.

The door was opened and they were thrown inside. Zak stumbled and fell. He heard the door clang shut. Switch knelt at his side, and helped him up. Zak's head seethed with a white-hot fury. He stared at Switch.

"He doesn't remember," he said with icy control. "He killed my parents and he doesn't even remember."

"I know," said Switch. "We'll get him, don't worry."

"How?" asked Zak. "How will we get him, Switch? It's all gone wrong. Cat and the others are dead . . ."

"We don't know that for sure," said Switch. He stopped speaking suddenly and his head turned sharply. "You!"

he gasped.

Zak spun round. A man was sitting on the floor at the far end of the room, watching them intently. Zak knew the man's face, but it was a few moments before he was able to place him.

It was the dark-haired man from the motorboat – the man who had warned them off when they had been snorkelling in Kharkhinos Cove.

The man stood up. "Project 17?" he asked.

Zak stared at him. Where was the heavy Greek accent? The man sounded English.

"What's Project 17 when it's at home?" asked Switch. "And who exactly would you be?"

The man ran light-footed to the door and pressed his ear against it, listening intently. Then he turned, looking the two of them up and down. "Why did Icarus fall?" he asked.

Zak heard Switch catch his breath.

"Because he flew too near the sun," Zak responded. It was the passcode that Colonel Hunter had taught them. Slingshot's passcode. Zak swallowed hard. He felt dizzy, as if his legs were about to give way.

"Jason?" he murmured.

The man's eyes narrowed. "How do you know my name?"

Zak stared into the man's dark eyes. His stomach was knotted. His throat was so tight he could hardly breathe. "I'm Zak," he said in a choking voice. "I'm your brother."

The man stared at him blankly. Then something ignited in his eyes. Hope? Disbelief? Recognition? Astonishment?

All the above.

And more.

"You look just like my old school photographs," he murmured. "Oh my God!"

Zak felt tears of overwhelming joy pricking his eyes. He clenched his fists, fighting to control himself. The very last thing he wanted was to break down in front of his brother and Switch and look like a total idiot.

"I visited Mum in the hospital," Jason murmured, gazing at Zak but sounding as though he was talking to himself. "Dad took me. She was sitting up in bed, holding the new baby." He shook his head. "Weirdest-looking thing I'd ever seen." He paused, as though swamped by memories. "She said they were having trouble coming up with the right name. I said you looked like a Zak."

"Good call," said Zak, a thick lump in his throat. "That's me."

Zak wasn't quite sure how, but suddenly he and Jason were hugging one another tightly. So tightly that for a few moments nothing else existed but the two of them. Reunited at last.

Wildcat crawled behind a broad tree, flattening herself into the ground, trying to ignore the intense pain in her arm. She could hear the rustle of someone moving quickly, coming closer.

She dragged herself to her feet, leaning heavily against the tree, taking deep breaths. She felt faint and sick and stinging sweat was running into her eyes. She held her breath, preparing herself to fight.

Taekwondo knifehand strike. Known in training as *sonkal taerigi.*

A twig cracked. A shape came around the tree. Cat flung out her arm, her hand rigid at throat height. The side of her hand made perfect contact with the carotid sinus at the side of the man's neck. He went down without a murmur.

She stooped and picked up his automatic machine gun. She moved off. Cautious. Her wounded arm hanging limp, blood threading down inside her sleeve and dripping off her fingers.

She saw a shape gliding along under the trees in the dark.

"Moon?"

"Cat?"

"Yes."

Moon ran towards her. Her eyes widened. "You're hurt." She quickly examined Cat's wound. "That needs bandaging," she said. She pulled Cat into the cover of an overhang of ground then took out a small pocket knife and tore off a strip of her shirt.

Cat winced as Moon tied the makeshift bandage around her upper arm.

"Sorry," Moon murmured.

"I can't believe how much it hurts," Cat said between gritted teeth. "Have you seen Hammer?"

"Not for a while," said Moon. She checked her Mob. It was zero-four-forty-five. "He'll be fine," she said. "You know Hammer. It'll take more than a few maniacs with machine guns to worry him."

"How do you think Switch and the others are doing?" Cat asked.

"If everything went to plan, they should be inside Base Hades by now," Moon said.

Cat winced as the pain flared through her arm again. "I hope so," she said.

"Come on," said Moon, helping Cat up. "I think our job here is done. Let's find Hammer and get out. "

*

Zak sat listening to his brother. He was trying hard to focus on what Jason was saying. He still felt dazed by the circumstances of their reunion.

He'd pictured their first moments together a thousand times in his head. But he'd never imagined anything like this. Locked up together by a power-crazed lunatic who was about to kill everyone in London in his quest to take over the world. It was beyond overwhelming. It was shredding his brain.

They had given Jason a quick run-down of the failed plan. He already knew how soon Achilles Rhea intended to fire the SWORD weapon.

There was maybe an hour to go before the Awakening of Perses – possibly less. They had no way of knowing how quickly time was passing. No Mobs, no weapons. Nothing. And a steel door between them and any hope of stopping it from happening.

Switch had wanted to know how Jason had ended up in a locked room in Base Hades.

"I created a vacancy in Rhea's organization," Jason explained. "I wanted to be as close to him as possible. He uses the motorboat all the time to shuttle between the islands."

"What do you mean, you created a vacancy?" Zak asked.

Jason looked at him. "Rhea had a guy who drove his motorboat," he said. "I met up privately with the driver and I managed to persuade him to seek alternative employment."

Zak blinked at him. "Oh."

He decided he didn't want to go into what methods of persuasion Jason had used. Best not to know.

"How did your cover get blown?" asked Switch.

"They caught me trying to disable the SWORD device," Jason said. "I thought if I could mess with its workings, that would give the good guys more time to locate and destroy this place."

Jason got up and began pacing around the room, as though too full of frustrated energy to keep still.

Like me, Zak thought, watching him. *He's just like me!*

Suddenly Jason let out a snarl of frustration and ran for the door. He landed a high side kick on the steel panel. The clang of the strike echoed through the room. The door held.

Jason stood staring at the door, his body vibrating with rage. He turned, and Zak was surprised at the calm expression on his face.

"We can't just sit here," Jason said with a cool determination. "Now there are three of us, we have more of a chance of putting a stop to this thing. We have to try and get out."

Zak looked around. The wall with the door in it was a sheet of steel. The other walls were solid rock. "How?" he asked softly. "Chew our way out with our teeth?"

"Can either of you fake screams of pain?" asked Jason. "I mean, the kind of screams you'd let out if you were dying in here?"

Switch and Zak both got to their feet. "We can try," Switch said. "You're hoping a guard will open the door to check it out? Do you think anyone will care enough to do that?"

"Rhea is a total psycho," said Jason. "But most of his men are just ordinary people – mercenaries – in it for the money. They're not crazy. If they think someone's dying in here, I think they'll open the door. Then we rush them." His eyes gleamed. "There was no point in me trying something like this on my own – they'd just have overwhelmed me. But the three of us can do it if we stick together. Are you with me?"

"All the way," said Switch.

Zak nodded.

He wondered how many armed men stood between them and SWORD.

Too many. We'll be killed, for sure.

But Zak couldn't quite get his head around the idea of dying.

No. Dying in this stone tomb wasn't an option.

Switch wasn't going to die down here – no way. And neither would he – not now he'd be fighting side by side with his brother.

Jason leaned against the door, listening again.

A sudden thump on the outside of the door made him jerk back, startled.

"What was that?" Switch asked.

There was a second thump. Something was being slammed against the other side of the door. Then there was a moment of silence before they heard a rattle of keys.

Jason leaped to the side of the door, bracing himself, his hands lifted in a martial arts pose.

The door opened.

"Dodge!" gasped Zak as a familiar figure appeared in the doorway. Dodge had a guard in a neck-lock. The man's face was purple.

"Don't!" cried Switch, as Jason made to attack. "He's with us! This is the guy we told you about."

Dodge dragged the struggling man over the threshold. "Shut the door," he said sharply.

Jason swung the door to.

Dodge shoved the man to the floor and knelt on his chest, leaning so that his mouth was close to the man's ear. Zak saw Dodge's lips moving rapidly. After a few seconds the man stopped struggling and lay staring up at Dodge with fear in his eyes.

"What did you say to him?" gasped Zak.

"I told him how many bones there are in the human hand," Dodge said coldly. "And how it would feel to have them all broken one by one."

Zak had never seen this side of Dodge. It was alarming – but it was also kind of awesome in a terrifying way.

Dodge squatted over the man. He pressed his forefinger to the man's windpipe. "If I press down here, it'll break your hyoid bone and you'll die of asphyxiation," he said with deadly calm. "Now, tell me exactly where the SWORD device is located and you'll live."

The man mumbled something that wasn't in English.

"He's Turkish," said Jason, crouching at Dodge's side.

"Did he understand anything I said to him?" asked Dodge.

"He got your general drift," said Jason. "But not the specifics." He spoke a few words to the man that Zak assumed must be Turkish.

The man answered rapidly, his eyes bulging.

Jason nodded and stood up. "Got it," he said. "He's too scared to be lying."

"Let's take him out of the game," said Dodge. "Silver? Switch? Get the guy's shoes and socks off. We'll tie him with the shoelaces and gag him with the socks."

Dodge tucked the man's automatic weapon under his arm as the four of them stepped into the corridor, leaving the guard bound and gagged on the floor.

Jason closed the door and turned the key. "Follow me," he said. "It's not far."

Zak was feeling stunned and elated. Things had turned around so quickly he was having trouble coming to terms with it.

The mission was back on course. With Switch and Dodge and Jason at his side, what could possibly go wrong?

Reaperman – you are so done for.

"What made you come for us?" Switch asked Dodge as they made their way along the corridor.

"I suppose you'd call it instinct," said Dodge. "You'd been gone too long without anything happening. I came inside and collared a guard. He spilled the beans. The problem is, I don't have any more explosives – Switch was carrying it all."

"They took my bag when they threw me in the cell," said Switch. "We need to find it." He glanced at the weapon under Dodge's arm. "One MP 5K submachine gun isn't going to get the job done."

"Indeed, it isn't." The deep gravelly voice seemed to come from all around them. "In fact, unless you wish to die where you stand, I would recommend you put the weapon down and raise your hands. Immediately, please, gentlemen."

Zak glanced up and saw a speaker high on the wall. That was where Rhea's voice was coming from. Next to it was a closed circuit camera. Pointing right at them.

There was the rapid clang of boots on the steel floor. Five men with automatic weapons appeared. They came to a halt and aimed their guns straight at Zak and the others.

Dodge put his gun on the floor and held up his hands.

Zak and the others did the same.

CHAPTER **ELEVEN**

FORTRESS.
BRIEFING ROOM P.17.L.02.
LOCAL TIME: 03:45

Colonel Hunter's face was grey with fatigue, but his eyes were keen and clear as he stared up at the digital clock display above the huge plasma screen.

It was showing Greek time.

On the island of Panos, it was zero-five-forty-five. In fifteen minutes, Reaperman would trigger SWORD and The Awakening of Perses would begin.

Colonel Hunter had no idea whether the deadly sonic wave from the device would penetrate this deep under the ground. He didn't much care. If the entire population of London was going to be killed, his own survival wasn't exactly a priority.

He was wearing an earpiece. He was in constant contact with the Home Secretary.

Bug was sitting at a desk with a laptop open.

"Anything?" the Colonel barked.

"Nothing," said Bug. He looked scared. But the Colonel had given him the chance to get out before zero hour. He had chosen to stay. As had all the other agents in Fortress.

"Do you have contact with your agents on Panos, Colonel?" came the Home Secretary's voice in the Colonel's ear.

"No, Ma'am," he replied. "Nothing for two hours now. That's not necessarily bad news, though. They could have gone dark to avoid detection. My people know what they're doing. Have you managed to persuade the Royals to leave the city?"

There was a protocol set up for evacuating the Royal Family in case of an emergency like this. A tunnel led from Buckingham Palace to Charing Cross tube station. From there a commandeered train would take them to London City Airport and away.

"They are not prepared to do that," said the Home Secretary. "Most of the Cabinet have been evacuated, but the Prime Minister is at Downing Street, awaiting word from us."

Colonel Hunter glanced again at the clock.

05:48.

There was still time.

"Bug?"

"No, Control. Nothing."

Colonel Hunter was glad he hadn't been the one forced to decide whether or not to warn Londoners of the impending attack. That terrible choice had been made at top government level after international consultation. The decision: the people should not be told. Even if they had started evacuating the city the moment Reaperman's deadline was known, the chaos and confusion would have meant gridlock and panic on the streets. A city the size of London could not be cleared in time.

But there was another reason for not broadcasting an alert – a reason that the Colonel knew must have wrenched the hearts of everyone involved. If the call had gone out to empty London, Reaperman would have learned of it. And then, what was to stop him re-programming SWORD, aiming its deadly beam at another great city?

London spared. The people of Paris wiped out. Or Kinshasa, or New York or Beijing or Moscow.

No. London had to remain the target. And everyone's hopes had to rest on Slingshot and Sergeant Carter and the small team of agents from Project 17.

"At what point do we assume the worst, Colonel?" asked the Home Secretary.

"At one second past zero-four-hundred, Ma'am," replied the Colonel. "My team has my full confidence until then."

"Very well,' said the Home Secretary. "I am going to contact the International Committee. I want the Failsafe team on full alert."

"Understood," said the Colonel.

The line went dead.

"Bug? Anything?"

Bug shook his head.

It was ten minutes to four, London time.

Six hundred seconds to zero hour.

Zak and the others were led along several corridors and up a number of flights of metal steps. The guards kept far enough back to prevent anyone from taking them by surprise. Even Zak couldn't move fast enough to avoid a spray of bullets from an automatic machine gun.

It was obvious that they were well above sea level now, climbing through caverns and tunnels and stairways cut from the solid rock of the hill that overlooked Kharkhinos Cove.

They came to a stretch of corridor that Zak was sure he recognized. It was lit by bright, glaring halogen strips. The walls were roughly hacked from stone. The floor was steel mesh. There were no doors leading off it, and at the far end there was a steel entrance with a round glass panel in it.

This was the corridor that led to the domed room which housed the SWORD device.

Zak remembered the face of the murdered Russian agent. He felt physically sick. He swallowed hard, fighting his fear.

The door opened. Dr Zoli stood there, smiling the same cold, thin, lizard smile that Zak had found so repellent in Agent Isabel's video.

"Welcome to my little domain," said Zoli, stepping aside so that the four prisoners were able to enter the chamber beyond the door.

It was exactly as Zak remembered, except that in real life the SWORD device looked bigger and stranger and more alarming than in the video.

The door opened onto a steel gallery which looked over a circular chamber. SWORD dominated the room, pivoting on its three heavy steel legs, its tubular muzzle pointing at the grey metal dome. A team of nine or ten people in white coats worked the electronic devices that lined the walls. LED lights blinked and pulsed. There was the soft constant whining of electronics as the white-coats moved about, consulting tablet computers, making tiny adjustments.

One man stood facing the SWORD device, his hands gripping the rail of the gallery, a blissful smile on his face.

Achilles Rhea – Reaperman – beamed with joy as he gazed at the monstrous machine that he was about to unleash on the innocent people of London.

There were plasma screens high on the walls under the dome. All alive. A face stared from many of them. European faces, African faces, Asian faces. Agents of World Serpent, Zak guessed, looking in on Reaperman's creation from all points of the globe. Waiting for the show to begin.

The other screens displayed scenes of a busy city. A railway station in the morning rush hour. People walking quickly along pavements. Massing at a kerb, waiting for traffic lights to change. Swarming across the road. Heavy traffic stopping and starting.

Zak realized with a sickening lurch that he was looking at live feeds from London. He recognized Waterloo Bridge. Trafalgar Square. Oxford Street. It all looked horribly ordinary. Horribly unsuspecting.

Why hadn't they evacuated the people? Warned them. Get out! Get out of there! Now!

"Ah, my friends, you are all here," Reaperman called to them. "And what superb timing!" He gestured towards a digital clock display.

05:52.

"You are about to witness something truly remarkable," he said. "You are privileged enough to be here for the death of one era and the birth of another." He turned to speak to a man standing behind him. "Open the dome, please. It's almost time."

Dr Zoli slithered away to check some terminals and displays.

There was a creaking, grinding sound from above. Zak looked up. The dome was opening like the iris of a camera. A circle of pale blue sky became visible at the very top.

"Awake, Perses," called Rhea. "And cover your eyes." He took a pair of sunglasses from his breast pocket and put them on. "It is going to get very bright in here."

Dr Zoli and the other white-coats put dark glasses on, then several of the white-coats pressed buttons and raised faders and turned dials. The electronic humming grew louder. Dr Zoli moved rapidly from bank to bank, checking that all was well.

Jason lurched forwards. "You'll be hunted down!" he said angrily. "The countries of the entire world will use all their resources to hunt you down and bring you to justice."

Two men dragged him back. A third hammered a gun butt into his stomach. He doubled up. Zak winced, struggling against the hands that held him.

"You're quite wrong," Rhea said calmly. "The governments of the world will do exactly as I wish. They will be too terrified to do otherwise. My beautiful SWORD will fill them all with . . . what do the Americans say? Shock and awe. They will capitulate to me or face annihilation."

"You'd kill millions of innocent people without a second thought?" spat Switchblade.

"That's exactly what I'd do," said Rhea. "My dear young man, to get what I want, I'd kill billions. I already have my next target in mind if the nations of the world prove reluctant to do as I demand. I will bring the blade of SWORD down on Tokyo. It has a population of over thirteen million."

"Mr Rhea?" called Dodge in a clear, controlled voice. "Your employees do know the truth about you, don't they?"

Rhea looked puzzled and mildly amused.

"What do you mean?" he asked.

"They do know that you're stark staring mad."

The amusement was wiped from Rhea's face. "Silence him!" he shouted, his face twisted in anger.

Fists and machine-gun butts beat Dodge to the ground. Rhea's face cleared as he watched Dodge being attacked. He smiled as he turned back to the great, humming device.

Switch and Zak fought to get free, but they were being held by too many men.

The dome was almost completely open now. The sky above the cavern was clear and blue. The electronic buzzing was growing rapidly louder and higher. The silver coils around SWORD's long tubular muzzle were beginning to glow.

The digital display showed 05:58.

LONDON.
FORTRESS.

Colonel Hunter stood behind Bug, his hands gripping the back of the boy's chair. Bug was typing rapidly on his laptop, trying to find some back-channel way of regaining contact with the team on Panos.

Whatever jamming devices Reaperman was using, they were good. Nothing Bug could come up with was able to penetrate them. Switch and the others were well and truly out of contact.

Bug was so caught up in his work that he hadn't noticed the time. Colonel Hunter had. His eyes were fixed on the Greek clock.

05:59.

Less than a minute to go.

The plasma screen was divided, showing a dozen different CCTV views of London. Teeming with people and traffic. A pleasant day. Blue skies.

Bug started as the Colonel's hand came down on his shoulder.

He looked up.

London time: 04:00.

Greek time: 06:00.

Time's up.

Wildcat was in a bad way. Moon had managed to support her as they climbed up through the forest, but with each step, it was getting more difficult. Cat's faltering feet stumbled over rocks and humps of earth and tree roots.

Moon paused. She hadn't heard any gunfire for a while now. She didn't know whether that meant Rhea's men had been called away or whether they were close by, stalking them in silence.

Moon looked at her Mob.

It was almost six o'clock.

Almost zero hour.

Had Dodge and the others succeeded? Or was SWORD about to be triggered? There was no way of knowing.

"Come on," she said to Cat, getting her shoulder up under her colleague's arm. "We have to keep moving."

Cat nodded, but the pain was making her woozy; she was finding it hard to think straight.

Just then a big figure came pushing through the trees.

"Hammer!" gasped Moon. "Thank God! Cat's been shot."

"I can see," said Hammer. "I'll take her. Come with me." He pointed back the way he had come. "There's something going on over there."

He took most of Wildcat's weight as they headed off through the trees.

Hammer led them to a break in the forest. A very strange sight met them. There was a round hump of land in an area clear of trees. But the summit of the hill was broken open and long triangular tongues of the ground had lifted and drawn back like the prongs of a crown. A high-pitched whining noise was coming from the hilltop.

They lowered Cat gently to the ground, then Moon followed Hammer up the scrubby hillside. The peeled-back sections turned out to be metal strips, camouflaged so that when they were closed, they looked like a natural part of the landscape.

The two agents crawled to the V-shaped gap between two of the segments. A stunning sight met their eyes.

They found themselves staring down into a huge cavern – staring straight at the business end of Reaperman's massive SWORD device. The coils around its long barrel were glowing with a fierce blue-white light.

Beyond the dazzle, they could just about make out some figures in white coats working at banks of electronic devices.

It seemed that Dodge and the others had failed. SWORD was operational. It was about to fire. Now it was down to the two of them.

Moon put her mouth to Hammer's ear.

"Got any PE4 left?" she asked.

Hammer nodded, pulling his backpack round and taking out a small chunk of the plastic explosive. He felt again in the pack and dug out a detonator and a small timing device.

The electronic whine was getting louder by the second. The light from the coils was blinding. Any second now the thing would trigger and its deadly beam would burst into the sky.

Hammer pressed the detonator into the PE4. There wasn't enough of the explosive to blow the entire device to pieces, but it should do enough damage to disable it – temporarily at least. His fingers shook as he attached the timer and set it for ten seconds.

Moon and Hammer looked at one another.

"Go for it," said Moon.

Hammer nodded and reached out over the open dome.

"Fire in the hold," he murmured as he flicked the timer on with his thumb and let go. Holding hands, they went careering down the hillside to where Wildcat was sitting and waiting for them.

"Down!" yelled Moon and they threw themselves flat against the ground.

CHAPTER **TWELVE**

Zak turned his head away, wincing in the flare of blue-white light, wishing he could cover his ears. The hum coming from the SWORD device had turned to a high, grating whine and the coils were burning with a blinding radiance.

Reaperman was standing at the rail of the gallery, his mouth half open, the brightness flashing off the lenses of his dark glasses. Dr Zoli had scuttled down a staircase to the ground below and he was moving rapidly round the SWORD device, checking that all the power cables were secure.

Zak wrenched against his captors' grip, but he couldn't get loose. Jason and Dodge were still on the metal floor of the gallery, Switch was being held against the wall, a forearm under his chin, his face contorted with hatred and rage.

Then, from the corner of his eye, Zak noticed something fall into the chamber. Small. Dark. Like a little chunk of rock that had come loose from above the dome.

It bounced off SWORD's coils and spun off towards the floor. Dr Zoli strode round SWORD's stumpy tripod legs to see what the thing was. He stooped over it and reached down.

He was caught in a fierce explosion. Zak saw him lifted off his feet and flung across the room in a ball of red flame.

Reaperman let out a furious yell, falling back as a fist of black smoke punched upwards.

Someone must have thrown a bomb down through the open dome. But the bomb had ricocheted off SWORD and exploded too far away to damage the device. The coils burned through the rising smoke, and the whine was still growing as the reverberations of the explosion died away.

It had to be Moon's team. That was *awesome!* They must be alive after all, and they were making a last attempt at putting SWORD out of action.

Zak felt a sudden surge of adrenaline flood through his body. Knowing that they were not alone had triggered a change in him. He was bursting with power and his brain was clear and razor-sharp.

He was in the zone.

Zak flung his legs out in front of him. His feet struck the top of the gallery rail, giving him the extra momentum he needed to flip completely over, ripping himself out of the hands of the three men surrounding him. Landing on his feet behind them, he kicked one in the back of the knee, driving him to the ground with a cry. The second man lunged at him, but Zak dived aside and the man crashed face first into the wall. He caught the third with a hammerfist strike to the chin. The man's head snapped back and he dropped like a stone.

Zak bounded up onto the narrow gallery rail, running along it, one foot planted with expert precision in front of the other, his arms out for balance as he sped away.

He had a specific target in mind.

He'd seen one of the white-coats do something when Reaperman had called for the dome to be opened. The man had twisted a small lever to one side.

Zak was aiming for that lever.

"Stop him!" howled Reaperman. "Bring him down!"

Bullets whined around Zak's ears, striking off the walls and rattling on the metal.

"No! Fools!" shrieked Reaperman. "No guns! You'll damage SWORD."

Zak was almost at the electronic bank with the lever. A man jumped in front of him, snatching at him with both hands. Zak leapfrogged over him, using his head as a springboard, and hit the lever at speed, yanking it back.

He heard the grinding and creaking noise as the dome began to close again. Reaperman turned, his face furious. Zak was ready for him — he was so in the zone now that his enemy seemed to be moving in slo-mo.

Zak spun round, rotating his hips, rising onto the ball of his foot, lifting his leg high and striking Reaperman in the side. Reaperman grunted in pain, doubling up so that he made himself a perfect target for a powerful palm-heel strike to the face.

Reaperman crashed to the ground at Zak's feet. It took all of Zak's willpower not to keep hitting the man as he sprawled face down on the floor. He was aware of chaos erupting all around him. White-coats were scattering in panic. Switch and Dodge and Jason had got free and were fighting back.

Zak grabbed one of the scientists. "How do I shut it off?" he yelled. But the man tore himself free and ran for the stairs. The sound of the SWORD device had risen to a maniacal shriek now and the pulsing light was blazing off the rapidly closing dome.

We have to get out of here!

Zak ran past the fleeing scientists, heading for the door. The white-coats were mostly heading for the stairway to ground level – he guessed there must be other exits down there. Jason and the others had almost dealt with all the guards. The last one went down from a karate chop from Jason just as Zak reached them.

Dodge already had the door open.

"Come on!" he shouted. "It's about to blow!"

Switch dived through the door. Dodge was right behind him. Jason grabbed Zak's arm and they went through together. Dodge snatched the door closed. They stared in through the round porthole.

A jet of blue-white light flashed upwards from the SWORD device, but they couldn't hear the electronic screeching any more. The door must be soundproofed. The deadly ray reflected down off the closed dome, flashing around the room like trapped lightning. A terrified face appeared at the inside of the window.

Achilles Rhea. His mouth stretched in a silent scream.

As Zak and the others watched in mute horror, blood began to pour from his eyes and nose. His hands clawed at the glass. Blood gushed from his mouth, spattering the glass as he slid away.

Zak looked away. It was a horrible way to die.

"Let's move," said Jason. "I don't think that machine was designed to work in an enclosed space."

They ran down the long corridor.

"Back to the hatch," said Dodge as they raced helter-skelter down a stairway. "We can get out under water."

"How come we're not dead?" asked Zak. "SWORD went off – why didn't it do the jelly-brain thing to us?"

"It was silent once the door was closed," said Jason. "My guess is that Rhea had that whole room proofed against the sonic waves getting through. In case of accidents while they were testing it."

"Lucky for us," said Switch.

"Lucky for us if we get out of here in one piece," said Dodge.

They heard a low rumbling noise from behind. The stairway shook. Dust rained down from the roof.

"I think it's overloading," said Jason. "There's no one in there to turn it off."

An explosion reverberated down the stairway. They heard the rumble and crash of falling rock and the shrill screech of twisted metal. A man's voice called out in fear, stopping short.

Dust came billowing down the stairs.

Zak and the others pelted along a corridor to the next flight – mayhem and death chasing in their wake.

"The thing is still active in there," shouted Moon, jumping to her feet. "Hammer – what else have you got?"

"Nothing," said Hammer. "That was it."

Moon shoved her hand into her backpack. She pulled out a single whizzer. Useless, she knew, but she had to try.

She scrambled back up the hill. Wildcat struggled to her feet and stumbled after her, Hammer right behind.

The light coming from the dome was so bright now that it was like staring into the sun. But as Moon came closer to the broken-open summit of the hill, the light began to fade. There was a grinding noise – metal grating against metal. The beam of light narrowed then blinked out. At the same time, the raised wedges of metal began to swing forward, slamming together to form a natural-looking hilltop again. A sudden strange quiet descended.

The three agents stood on the hump of land, staring at one another.

"I don't get it," said Hammer. "Why have they closed it? Did the thing fire? Is it over?"

"I don't think so," said Wildcat, cradling her wounded arm. "I think something's gone seriously screwy down there." She looked at the other two. "The boys made it!" she said with a fierce grin. "Reaperman didn't do this – Switch and Silver did!"

"You think?" said Moon.

The hill trembled under their feet. There was a deep rumbling noise.

"I don't like it," said Moon. "Whoever did *what* down there, we need to be somewhere else."

Supporting Wildcat as best they could between them, Moon and Hammer raced back down the smooth hillside. There was another dull rumble that shook the ground.

"All hell's breaking loose in Base Hades," said Wildcat. "If this is down to Switch and Silver, I hope they get out okay."

They ran for the trees.

An explosion ripped through the hill, sending up a great burst of earth and rock and twisted metal.

The three agents flung themselves to the ground as the debris rained over them.

Base Hades was ripping itself to pieces around them as Zak and the others ran for the airlock room deep below. Explosions reverberated through Reaperman's underground headquarters. Roofs caved in moments after they passed; walls cracked and crumbled. Falling boulders punched holes in metal floors. Electronic devices sizzled and burst into flames.

At last they came back to that first small chamber. They flung themselves through the bulkhead door and Switch slammed it behind them a moment before the roof of the outer corridor came tumbling down.

The abandoned scuba gear was still lying on the floor by the open hatch. Dark water lapped the edges, spilling out and washing over the floor.

There was a fizzing noise and they were suddenly plunged into darkness. Whatever source supplied electricity to Base Hades had been taken out in the chaos.

"No one move," said Dodge.

Zak could hear his heart beating very fast in the pitch blackness. But he wasn't scared. Exhilarated, a bit freaked out, feeding off a massive adrenaline rush. Standing next to his *brother*.

A small light came on. Dodge had located the wrist-torch they'd left with the scuba gear. He shone the narrow beam at their faces.

"We won't need breathing gear," he said. "I'll go first and light the way to the hatch. Follow me, swim through and then head for the surface. It's not far."

He sat on the edge of the hole, swinging his legs down into the water. He gave a thumbs up and slid down out of sight. Zak could see the glow of the torch wavering under the circle of disturbed water.

Switch went next.

Zak and Jason briefly gripped each other's hands in the darkness.

"See you in a little while," said Jason. "Down you go."

Zak crouched by the hatch, then jumped into the water.

Zak burst to the surface, gulping in air as he swung his arms and trod water.

The sky was blue above the steep forested hillsides of Kharkhinos Cove. He could hardly believe it. After so long underground, the fresh air and daylight didn't seem real.

He spotted Switch's head bobbing in the water nearby. He swam towards him. Dodge was only a few metres away, staring up at something on the hill.

Zak turned to look. Achilles Rhea's villa was in flames.

Jason's head came shooting up. He pulled his hair out of his eyes.

"Base Hades is having a major meltdown," said Switch. "Shame!"

Zak even noticed the flicker of flames on the big black freighter.

"We're not safe yet," said Jason. "Rhea used that ship as a munitions store. It could go up any second."

Munitions. Explosives and weapons.

Big boom. Not good.

They swam as fast as they could for the far side of the inlet.

They were about halfway across when the freighter exploded. Hot shrapnel hit the water all around them, sizzling and smoking.

"Is everyone okay?" shouted Dodge.

"I'm fine," called Zak. He could see that Switch and Jason were also unhurt. The freighter was burning from prow to stern and already settling lower in the water. Huge clouds of black smoke were rising into the sky. The *Cerberus* was hidden in a ball of flames. Another plume of dark smoke was spiralling from beyond the high ridge of the hillside.

They swam to the far shore. There was a rocky beach under a canopy of trees. They dragged themselves out of the water and stood staring across the inlet at the flames that were pouring from the freighter and the villa.

Reaperman was dead. Base Hades was finished.

"Mission accomplished," Zak murmured, his hair dripping in his eyes. But he had no sense of triumph. The adrenaline rush had drained away now. He felt exhausted and shredded and numb. He saw Reaperman's blood-streaked face for a moment in his mind. He shuddered, pushing the horrible image away.

"What about Moon and the others?" said Switch. "Rhea said they were dead, but at least one of them must be alive – someone on our side threw that bomb into the SWORD room."

"You're right," said Dodge. "Let's hope they're all alive." He turned and scanned the steep hillside behind them. "We have quite a climb on our hands to get out of here," he said. "We need to find some place where there's a telephone or internet access so we can report back."

"I think they'll already know we were successful," said Jason. "It's zero hour plus some – and nothing will have happened in London." He turned to Zak. "We're quite the team, little brother," he said with a smile.

Zak nodded back, but there were too many conflicting emotions crashing about inside his head for him to be able to take in the reality of the situation yet. Reaperman was dead. SWORD had been destroyed. Base Hades was in flames. But what about Moon and Hammer and Wildcat? And what about all the other people who had been part of Reaperman's global terrorist organization? Would World Serpent just wither away and die now that Rhea was dead?

"What's that noise?" asked Switch. He was scanning the eastern sky, his hand shielding his eyes from the early morning sun.

They all listened. It was a steady rhythmic throbbing. Budda-budda-budda. Gradually getting louder.

"Look!" shouted Jason, pointing as a helicopter came gliding round the northern headland of Kharkhinos Cove.

They waved as the helicopter approached. It was green, with the letters S.A.R. on the side. Instead of the usual wheels, long sausage-shaped pontoons were fixed to the undercarriage.

"It's the good guys," said Jason as the helicopter swooped in. "It's an AS-332C1 Super Puma. That's Greek army."

The helicopter swept in, whipping the trees into a frenzy as it settled on the rippling surface of the water. Zak held his arm up over his face as the downdraught of the rotor blades tore at his wet clothes and raked through his hair.

The side door slid open.

"Hi, guys!" Moonbeam shouted above the noise of the engine. "Come on over. These guys are going to get us out of here."

Switch waded into the water. "What about Hammer and Cat?" he shouted.

"Get over here and you can ask them yourselves," shouted Moon. "Move it, guys! What are you waiting for – a written invitation?"

CHAPTER **THIRTEEN**

FORTRESS.
COLONEL HUNTER'S OFFICE.
FOUR DAYS LATER.

Zak sat facing Colonel Hunter's desk. The Colonel was reading the final page of the official report on Operation Icarus. Zak wasn't listening as carefully as his boss would have wished. He felt as if reality hadn't quite kicked in yet. As if this was still some kind of dream. Jason was in a chair on his left-hand side and Dodge was on the other. He was sitting there sandwiched between his best friend and his brother.

How cool was that?

Zak gave his brother a sidelong glance. He couldn't get over how alike they were. Jason had the same colour hair as him – and he used gel that made it stand up in a spiky spray just like he did. The startled cockatoo effect, as Jackhammer called it. They had the same eyes. Their mother's eyes, Jason had told him, passed on to them along with her stubbornness and her moral code. They'd inherited their sense of humour and fun from their father.

Janet and John Trent's two sons, sitting in a secret complex thirty metres under London. Both working as agents of British Intelligence, both following in their mother's footsteps.

So cool!

Zak looked at Dodge. Former SAS Sergeant Tony Carter was dressed in a smart navy-blue suit and a red silk tie. Clean-shaven, hair trimmed and brushed. Zak had to admit his down-and-out friend cleaned up very well, but he was finding Dodge's change of appearance a little tricky to get his head around. For the time being Dodge was living in a hotel room in central London paid for by MI5. But then what? Back under the arches at Waterloo Station? Surely not.

Colonel Hunter's voice drifted back into his mind. "The internationally co-ordinated Failsafe team, led by a helicopter squadron of the Hellenic Airforce, took the Project 17 agents off the island, along with MI5 Field Agent Slingshot, and Anthony Carter, serving as temporary sergeant under my command," read the Colonel. "They were flown to Araxos Air Base. Agent Wildcat had suffered ballistic trauma to her upper right arm and was airlifted to the 409 army hospital in Patras."

Ballistic trauma? Oh – he means she was shot.

"The wound was treated and she was discharged at ten-hundred hours the following morning. All British operatives involved in Icarus returned to the UK the same day."

Colonel Hunter glanced up from the file. "I've added a codicil at the end," he said. He looked down and began reading again. "Operation Icarus would not have been successful without the expertise and assistance of Anthony Carter, who came willingly out of retirement for this mission. If he so wishes, I firmly recommend he be given appropriate employment either in the military or Intelligence Services."

Dodge leaned forward. "Thank you, Colonel, but I could never go back to that life. I helped this once. But that's it for me."

"But you can't go back on the streets, surely?" Zak said anxiously. "That's crazy, Dodge. Seriously! You'll have no money or anything."

Dodge smiled. "Poor and content is rich enough, Zachary," he said. "But I won't be going back on the streets. With the money I was paid for my work in Operation Icarus I'll be able to start a new life." He smiled, resting his hand on Zak's shoulder. "In fact, I've already found a small house in the New Forest. I've made some enquiries and I'm going to be working as a wildlife ranger."

Zak gazed at him in delighted amazement. "Way to go, Dodge!" he said. He frowned. "Or should I call you something else now?"

"Dodge works for me," he said. "And my house is in a small town with a railway link to London – so we can still see each other." He glanced at Colonel Hunter. "When you have the time, of course."

The Colonel closed the Operation File and stood up, extending his hand across the desk towards Dodge. "I'd like to thank you again for your assistance, Mr Carter," he said as Dodge got up and took his hand. "If I can ever be of help, you know how to contact me." He glanced at Zak and there was a twinkle in his eye. "Although strictly speaking, you shouldn't."

"You can trust me, Colonel," said Dodge.

"I'm well aware of that, Mr Carter," Colonel Hunter replied. "But I'm afraid we have some pressing business now. My secretary Ms Farris will show you out." He turned to Zak and Jason. "We're needed in Briefing Room P.17.L.O2. Some new information has come through from Panos."

All the agents from Operation Icarus were in the main briefing room, along with Jason, Colonel Hunter, Bug and a couple of sci-tech people from Research and Development. Wildcat's arm was in a sling and Moon and Hammer had some small cuts and bruises from where the hillside had exploded, but otherwise everyone was fine.

They were watching a live video feed from Base Hades. A team had been sent in there to check on the damage.

From what Zak could see, the place was a total wreck. Floodlights moved over rooms and corridors where pieces of twisted and mangled metal stuck up out of heaps of rubble. The agent working the camera was breathless from the exertion of getting around in there.

"We've found and removed fifty-two bodies so far," he said. "It's not pleasant down here, I can tell you. From what we can make out, not much has survived. The Failsafe Team picked up another thirty-five men who escaped the Base. They're in prison on the mainland now, awaiting trial."

"Have you reached the chamber where the SWORD device was housed, Agent Blackwater?" asked Colonel Hunter.

"We think so," said Blackwater. "But it's full of rubble – we can't get in there yet. It'll be days before we can make an assessment."

"Has the machine been destroyed?" asked Jason.

"That's an affirmative," said Blackwater. "Nothing could have survived in there. Our forensic people think the whole series of explosions and fires started when the device overloaded and blew up."

"I can vouch for that," said Hammer. "A great big lump of it nearly took my head off!"

"You have no absolute confirmation that Reaperman is dead?" asked the Colonel. "No body?"

"I doubt there'll be a body to find, sir," said Blackwater. "Everything in there was mashed to a pulp from what I've seen so far. But there's some positive news. We found a room in the villa that wasn't destroyed in the fire that gutted the rest of the place. It was metal-sheathed – presumably for security. There's some heat damage but the computer terminals are intact. We're having them shipped out to be properly investigated. One of the tech guys I spoke to says there's information on there about the entire global network of World Serpent. With any luck, we'll have the whole lot of them in the bag before too long, sir."

"That's good news, Agent," said the Colonel. "Keep your team safe in there. Fortress out."

The vid-link was broken. An aerial scene of Panos took its place on the huge plasma screen as a helicopter roved over the hills to the north of Kharkhinos Cove. Zak leaned forwards. Thin smoke still rose from the burned-out and half-sunk hulk of the black freighter. The *Cerberus* wasn't visible. Zak guessed it must have gone to the bottom – to lie alongside that other sunken boat they had seen. The one they had assumed belonged to the Russian agent who was killed. There was some justice in that.

High on the hillside, a patch of forest was burned back from the ruined villa. Zak could just make out some people in protective clothing moving about among the charred remains. Further from the inlet there was an open space in the forest with a deep circular hole punched into it: the only visible remains of the domed chamber that had housed SWORD.

Colonel Hunter clicked a remote and the screen went blank. All eyes turned to him. "The international committee responsible for the global hunt for the terrorist organization known as World Serpent has asked me to convey their appreciation for your work on Operation Icarus," he said.

"Nice to be appreciated," said Switch with a grin.

"Indeed," said the Colonel dryly. "You all did your jobs very well – which is exactly what I would expect from you."

"So, what happens now, Control?" asked Moon. "Do we get a few down days as a reward?"

"A holiday," murmured Hammer. "That would be sweet."

"Once you have handed in your written reports, I'll consider all applications for leave," said the Colonel. "But don't be fooled, Agents. World Serpent was not the only dangerous organization out there. And Reaperman was not the only man capable of global terrorism."

"Like the Lernaean Hydra, huh, Control?" said Wildcat. "You know, the serpent in all that Greek mythology that Rhea was so keen on. Cut off the Hydra's head and two more will take its place."

Zak looked at her. Cat was like some kind of walking encyclopedia. But he really didn't like the idea of new people taking over where Reaperman left off.

"Is that going to happen, Control?" he asked.

"If it does, I will expect my Project 17 agents to acquit themselves as well as they did in Operation Icarus," said the Colonel. "You may go about your business now. Remember, reports on my desk in forty-eight hours. Dismissed."

There was something Zak still needed to know. He lifted his hand.

"Of course, no briefing would ever be complete without a final question from Quicksilver," said the Colonel with a quick smile. "How can I help you, Agent?"

"Do you have any information about Agent Isabel?" Zak asked. He had last seen her driving off at breakneck speed over the foothills of the Atlas Mountains with a whole bunch of Reaperman's men on her tail.

The Colonel nodded. "I received a report from the German BND that she returned to base two days ago," he said. "You have nothing to worry about, Quicksilver – Agent Isabel is fine."

Zak let out a sigh of relief. Isabel had survived. That was great news.

"And now," said the Colonel. "With Agent Quicksilver's permission, you are all dismissed."

Jason had his arm across Zak's shoulder as they started to file out. The Colonel got them to wait until the others had gone.

"I'm going to try and arrange for the two of you to spend some free time together," he said. He smiled at Zak. "You did good work on Panos, Agent," he said. "Your parents would be proud of you – *both* of you."

TWO DAYS LATER.
THE LONDON EYE.
JUBILEE GARDENS.

Zak and Jason stood side by side, gazing out over the panorama of London as the pod they were in lifted slowly into the sky. It was a fine, sunny day and the winding river glittered and sparkled below them.

Zak had handed in his written report first thing that morning. Control insisted the reports be submitted in hard copy as well as computer file. Zak assumed it was because the Colonel was so old – he still liked things to be on paper.

Zak was almost getting used to being with his brother. Almost. He'd wake up in the morning and think perhaps it had all been a dream. Then he'd meet up with Jason in the canteen and things would be so normal and natural between them that it was as if they'd never been apart.

"I've heard from my division commander," said Jason.

Excitement bubbled through Zak. "About you coming to work in London?" he asked. That had been Zak's hope for the past few days – the idea that they'd be together permanently, that he might even get to work with Jason now and then.

"I told you that wasn't very likely," said Jason.

Zak's hopes tumbled. "They said no?"

Jason put his arm around Zak's shoulders. "They need me doing the job I'm best at, Zak," he said. "I'm sorry, but that's undercover work out in the field. You know that, don't you?"

Zak nodded glumly. "Yes, I know that," he said. "I just *hoped*, you know?"

There was silence between them for a few moments as the pod reached the summit of the Eye and the whole of London spread out before them.

"We'll have some more time before you go, won't we?" Zak asked.

"A little while," said Jason. "I leave on my next mission in five days' time."

Zak stared at him. "*Five days?*"

That wasn't anything like long enough. There was so

much stuff he wanted to tell Jason about, so much he wanted them to do together.

"Where are you going this time?" Zak asked quietly.

"That's classified, little brother," said Jason. "Sorry."

"How long for?" He looked up at Jason. "Classified?"

"I'm afraid so."

"Any chance that they'd let you take a speedy little sidekick along with you?" Zak asked.

"I don't think so." Jason smiled at him. "Anyway – how speedy are you, really? I haven't seen you running yet. Think you could beat me in a race?"

"With one foot tied behind my back," said Zak with a grin.

"No way," said Jason. "I'm pretty fast. I reckon I could outrun you, no problem."

"In your dreams!" said Zak, rising to the challenge. "Want to try it?"

"You are so on, Zak!" said Jason.

"The Millennium Arena's not far away," said Zak. "It's got a race track and everything. I hope you're a good loser."

"I don't know if I am or not," said Jason. "I've never lost."

Zak grinned from ear to ear. Loving this. "Well, let me introduce you to a brand new experience then."

"How about we make it a bit more interesting," said Jason. "If you beat me, I'll take you and your pals at Project 17 out for a slap-up meal tonight at the restaurant of your choice. How does that sound?"

"Expensive for you," said Zak.

"We'll see," said Jason, ruffling Zak's hair.

"Oh, trust me, big brother, we will!" said Zak. "We really will."

THE SAN HUNG RESTAURANT. SOHO, LONDON.

Jason had hired an entire room for the party. Wildcat was there, along with Switch and Moon and Jackhammer. Zak had even managed to coax Bug out of his little office for the evening. Colonel Hunter had politely declined Zak and Jason's invitation. He had a prior engagement with the Director General of MI5.

They were sitting at a huge circular table with a revolving tray loaded with bowls and plates of food. Everyone was trying chopsticks, often with results that had the rest of them yelling with laughter as food went skittering across the table or dropped into someone's lap.

Despite having her arm in a sling, Wildcat turned out to be the most adept with the sticks. Bug was hopeless and soon resorted to using a fork.

"So, how much did he beat you by?" Switch asked Jason as he tucked into kung pao chicken and egg fried rice.

"I really don't remember exactly," said Jason. "A few tenths of a second, I think."

"And the rest!" said Zak. "I went twice round the track while you were still warming up."

Hammer laughed. "He's a nippy little ferret, isn't he?" he said. "You should see him move when there's fried chicken in the canteen."

"I have to be fast in there, the way you shovel drumsticks onto your plate," said Zak. "No one else would get a look-in."

Moon tapped her glass with her chopsticks. "A toast!" she called. "Raise your glasses, please to our good friends and reunited brothers – Agents Quicksilver and Slingshot!"

"We're off-duty, I think we can call them by their real names just this once," said Switch.

"To Zak and Jason!" said Moon. There was a cheer and a clink of glasses.

Zak couldn't have been happier. He was with friends

and family. And when he thought of family, he didn't just mean Jason. These other people were just as much family to him now. Finally meeting up with Jason had been the most astounding thing in his life, but Project 17 and the friends he had made here *were* his life. He gazed around at them, blissfully happy.

Life really was amazing.

the orion star

Sign up for **the orion star** newsletter to get inside information about your favourite children's authors as well as exclusive competitions and early reading copy giveaways.

www.orionbooks.co.uk/newsletters

Follow on

Orion
Children's Books